Heart

&

Soul

By:

Brooke St. James

Other titles available from Brooke St. James:

Another Shot:
(A Modern-Day Ruth and Boaz Story)

When Lightning Strikes

Something of a Storm (All in Good Time #1)
Someone Someday (All in Good Time #2)

Finally My Forever (Meant for Me #1)
Finally My Heart's Desire (Meant for Me #2)
Finally My Happy Ending (Meant for Me #3)

Shot by Cupid's Arrow

Dreams of Us

Meet Me in Myrtle Beach (Hunt Family #1)
Kiss Me in Carolina (Hunt Family #2)
California's Calling (Hunt Family #3)
Back to the Beach (Hunt Family #4)
It's About Time (Hunt Family #5)

Loved Bayou (Martin Family #1)
Dear California (Martin Family #2)
My One Regret (Martin Family #3)
Broken and Beautiful (Martin Family #4)
Back to the Bayou (Martin Family #5)

Almost Christmas

JFK to Dublin (Shower & Shelter Artist Collective #1)
Not Your Average Joe (Shower & Shelter Artist Collective #2)
So Much for Boundaries (Shower & Shelter Artist Collective #3)
Suddenly Starstruck (Shower & Shelter Artist Collective #4)
Love Stung (Shower & Shelter Artist Collective #5)
My American Angel (Shower & Shelter Artist Collective #6)

Summer of '65 (Bishop Family #1)
Jesse's Girl (Bishop Family #2)
Maybe Memphis (Bishop Family #3)
So Happy Together (Bishop Family #4)
My Little Gypsy (Bishop Family #5)
Malibu by Moonlight (Bishop Family #6)
The Harder They Fall (Bishop Family #7)
Come Friday (Bishop Family #8)

So This is Love (Miami Stories #1)

3

All In (Miami Stories #2)
Something Precious (Miami Stories #3)

The Suite Life (The Family Stone #1)
Feels Like Forever (The Family Stone #2)
Treat You Better (The Family Stone #3)
The Sweetheart of Summer Street (The Family Stone #4)
Out of Nowhere (The Family Stone #5)

Delicate Balance (The Blair Brothers #1)
Cherished (The Blair Brothers #2)
The Whole Story (The Blair Brothers #3)
Dream Chaser (Blair Brothers #4)

Mischief & Mayhem (Tanner Family #1)
Reckless & Wild (Tanner Family #2)
Heart & Soul (Tanner Family #3)

Chapter 1

Stella Wilde

Lexington, Kentucky

Liam was acting differently when he came into our apartment that evening. I could see it right away. I was standing in the kitchen, waiting for water to boil so that I could make myself a cup of tea. I had a clear view of the door, and I was looking that way when Liam came inside.

His face fell as soon as our eyes met.

"What's the matter?" I asked.

It seemed as though he was disappointed about something. He started to speak to me, but then he just sighed. He turned away to take his shoes off by the door. He was forlorn, I could see that even with his back to me.

"What happened, Liam? What's the matter?"

"I'm coming," he said in a serious tone.

It was 9pm and I hadn't seen him all day. He had jury duty and then he went to his shared art studio space afterward. I wondered what could possibly have him so upset. Liam had a flair for drama, so I assured myself that his mood could be caused by something as little as feeling tired after a long day. He had a lot going on without jury duty, so I knew he would come home tired tonight.

Liam was an extremely talented visual artist and musician. He was an abstract painter, and when he wasn't creating art, he was busy practicing and performing with the symphony. He also modeled some, which was simply a product of how visually appealing he was. He wasn't a full-time model by any stretch of the imagination, but he had done some work for a local men's store and he was sponsored by a few small brands because of his social media following.

We had a friend named Nick who was a photographer and took artsy pictures of him playing music and painting and even doing mundane things like eating or getting out of the shower.

Liam was living his best life. He was modeling, playing music, and selling his art consistently. We were friends with enough artists to know that Liam was the exception to the rule. The phrase *starving artist* existed for a reason. Liam Alexander, however, was making it, living the dream.

I had a lot going on in my life as well.

The last six months had been extremely busy. I graduated in May, and now I was in my very first year as a first-grade school teacher. I was also a classically trained pianist who gave lessons to six students a week. I used to have more, but I had to cut back when my classroom turned out to be more difficult than I anticipated.

It was currently October, so I was only two months into the school year, and I was completely exhausted and overwhelmed most days when I got home. Turns out, managing a classroom of twenty-two first-graders was extremely hard work. It was challenging physically, mentally, and emotionally. I had a few children in my classroom with, let's just say, difficult personalities.

This was something that I knew to expect. I had done student teaching and received plenty of advice. I didn't think everything was going to be peachy, but I honestly hadn't anticipated that a few of the kids in my class would have blatant respect issues right off the bat. I had been hoping for the best during my first year, and so far, that was not happening.

I still had confidence that I would be able to work things out and settle into a more comfortable routine eventually, but for now, I was totally spent and frustrated in the evenings.

Tonight was no different. I was thoroughly exhausted. It was for this reason that I stared blankly at Liam's sulking profile as he took his shoes off. I honestly didn't care that he was in a weird mood. I was thankful he was home. I wanted to tell him about my day and make jokes with him about it. I was happy that I had someone like Liam to share life with—someone with whom I could let my guard down.

It seemed like he needed to do the same at this moment. I assumed he had as long of a day as I had.

"I saved you some leftovers from that Greek restaurant," I said as I absentmindedly poured hot water into my mug. "I picked it up a little while ago and I ordered extra for you."

I dunked the teabag, watching him, waiting for him to meet me in the kitchen.

Once he took off his jacket and scarf, he was left wearing all black. He walked toward me with that cautious, regretful expression that had me feeling a little wary. He was looking toward the side of me, into the kitchen, and I glanced over my shoulder to see what had caught his attention. Nothing was there, though. He just seemed to have a hard time making eye contact with me.

I stared at him, experiencing a sudden wave of dread at the thought that whatever was bothering him might be more serious than I anticipated.

I thought he would come into the kitchen to greet me or perhaps start eating the food I had mentioned, but he didn't. He stopped on the other side of the bar and took a seat on one of the stools.

"What's going on?" I asked, looking at him even though he hadn't made eye contact with me.

Liam took an unsteady breath and glanced at me regretfully before looking away again. "We need to talk," was all he said. His voice was breathy. He was nervous, and that increased my feeling of dread. I leaned onto the countertop, stretching to the side to try to get him to look at me.

"It's good news," he said in a sad but somewhat reassuring tone. "It's good for me, in a way, but it's bittersweet, too, obviously."

I had been with Liam for almost two years. We were together for over a year before I decided to move in with him. I knew him well, and I had never seen him behave this strangely.

"What happened?" I asked, staring at him. I felt like I was standing outside of my own body, staring at both of us.

He sighed again. "Well, I didn't even mention any of this to you because I didn't want to get my hopes up or anything, but Boston, Stella. You know how I've always loved Boston."

"What about Boston?" I asked.

"They want me!" he said in a breathy, mostly excited tone. "There's a gallery that's going to showcase my work, Stella. You know Heather that I met in Cincinnati? She works for that huge gallery in Boston. They're hooking me up with a month-long exclusive, and who knows what after that with all the new connections. I've already been talking to the people at the BSO. You know what a dream come true that would be for me. That's freaking amazing. I sent a link to my stuff, and they said I could have an audition."

Liam stopped talking and stared straight at me with an expression that was so full of different emotions I had no idea how he felt. He looked happy and sad and excited and freaked out all at the same time. His face kept subtly moving and changing.

"I'm moving to Boston, Stella. I have to do it. It's an opportunity I can't afford to miss. I'd be devastated with myself later in life if I didn't follow my dream. I have to go where my heart takes me, or my own mental health will suffer down the line. I have to watch out for those sorts of things. You know about my anxiety. I have triggers, and I can't cope with regret." He paused and breathed a long sigh.

My heart pounded, but his words and facial expressions were contradicting and confusing. I wasn't exactly sure what he was saying. I couldn't understand if we were moving, or we were breaking up or what was going on.

"Parts of it are absolutely going to kill me, though," he said. "You have no idea how hard it was for me to think about ending things with you."

"Why would you need to end things with me?" I asked, since it was the only logical question.

Liam didn't answer right away, and I felt a rush of something physical that was like hot and cold flashes happening at the same time. My stomach turned, and I suddenly felt nauseated.

"I'm moving to Boston, Stella."

He said the words so slowly and seriously that I knew he wasn't joking around.

I saw some regret in his expression, so I asked again, "Why would that mean you need to end things with me?"

"Because, Stella. I'm going up there. I'm moving. It's not temporary. It just can't work between us. It kills me to say that, but I just can't do it. I thought of everything, and I just think this is where our lives separate. We're going different directions. A long-distance relationship is out of the question. I hate this, but I'm leaving in a couple of weeks, so I have to get things sorted out."

He was speaking softly, and I was just delirious enough in that moment that I laughed.

Liam scowled at me like my laughter hurt him.

"What's going on here, Liam? I feel like you're joking."

"I'm not joking," he said, looking sad, hopeless.

"So, you're standing here seriously telling me we're breaking up?" I asked.

"Yes, Stella. I'm moving in two weeks," he said, looking serious and patient.

"Two weeks? That's not even an option. We just renewed the lease. We have nine months left on it."

"Both of us are on it now," he said, shaking his head like it wasn't a problem. "I knew with your job and family and everything, you'd be staying here. I won't even worry about taking my name off the lease. The landlords will never know the difference. I was paying for the place myself for a year before you moved in, so I knew you could cover it with your job and everything. Like I said, all the pieces just fell into place. I've kind of already thought of everything, and I'm just... right now I'm just in a spot where I can go. As hard as it is, I know it's the right thing."

He was talking about it in a business-like, detached manner. I was almost certain that he was breaking up with me but it was surreal how matter-of-fact he was. It definitely seemed like his mind was made up.

My thoughts raced in those seconds.

We had just renewed his lease three months ago when I moved in with him, and now he was saying he was leaving me. *Was that really what he was saying? That I should stay here and pay for the apartment alone while he packs up and moves to Boston?*

I honestly felt like this was all a big joke.

As I stared at Liam, I realized that his sorrowful expression was laced with a sort of barely hidden excitement or happiness.

This obviously made me feel enraged.

My cheeks and jaw felt hot and tight, and I fought desperately to hold back tears. I had that odd feeling that my entire life was about to change. I wasn't ready for this on a random Thursday night when I was already exhausted. Within seconds, I had gone from having a normal evening to feeling humiliated, scared, and heartbroken.

"It hurts me so bad, Stella," Liam said, shaking his head and staring at me seriously.

"Just don't do it if it hurts," I said.

Liam tilted his head to the side and made a face like he was confused by my statement. "I'm sorry, but I have to," he said. "I have to follow my dream. This is bittersweet for me, Stella."

"Are you really breaking up with me right now?" I asked, my voice shaking. I was surprised I could speak at all. I blinked at him, feeling dazed. I was stirred with so much emotion and adrenaline that my ears were ringing.

"I'm sorry, but it's just something I think we need to do. You're so focused on your job, and—"

"I'm focused on my job because I'm only two months into it, Liam. I was just thinking about that before you came in. Things aren't always going to be this crazy for me. I'll settle in."

"Either way," he said, shaking his head. "You're just starting out in your career, and I'm... I don't know. I'm starting mine, too, but I'm moving up. I'm going to need to travel and do things and go places."

He paused and stared at me like it was my turn to talk.

"Did you just say you're *moving up*? What does that mean?" I was fuming. I didn't even know where to begin.

Liam let out a little sigh. "I was just saying, I'm going to be really busy. I don't know if I have time for a relationship, necessarily. I don't think either of us need this. It's not just me. You're just as busy as I am."

I gawked at him, feeling absolutely stunned.

What I wanted to say was that a good, stable relationship was exactly what I needed. I needed him to be there for me after a long day. I had hoped that was what I was getting when I decided to move in with him.

"Please don't cry," he said, when tears began to roll down my cheeks.

It didn't happen until just now when it finally sunk in that he was completely serious.

Liam was breaking up with me.

Dumping me.

Leaving me.

Moving out.

I was completely blindsided by this moment.

It had come out of nowhere.

I was happy.

I thought we were both happy.

I wanted to be with Liam forever.

I thought that was the plan.

I would never have agreed to move in with him if I would have known this would happen.

I could understand that he wanted to move away from Lexington. He had talked about living in a bigger city one day. But I honestly couldn't believe he wanted to go without me. I couldn't fathom it. I put my hand over my face, closing my eyes and wishing I could go back in time and make this whole conversation go away.

I wanted to insist that Liam's name was on the lease and he legally couldn't just move out and leave me to pay the rent. I wanted to beg him to reconsider.

But I just held my tongue. I was extremely close to breaking down and begging him to stay, but whatever was left of my pride prevented me from doing so. My thoughts and emotions were so all over the map that I couldn't even figure out what to say next.

"What's supposed to happen now?" I asked, peering at him through my fingers.

"I was thinking I would spend the night at Kate and Collin's. I'll probably just stay over there until I move. Don't worry, I'll wait until you're at work to come get my stuff."

Chapter 2

I slept alone that night.

Technically, I didn't get much sleep, but I was alone in the apartment. I didn't talk to another soul after Liam left—not even on the phone. I was tempted to call one of my friends or my mother for some support, but I didn't.

I couldn't talk about it.

I couldn't even believe it was real.

Maybe I should have seen it coming.

Maybe it was my fault for being too busy and overwhelmed with work.

Either way, I was blindsided.

The anger, hurt, heartbreak, and anxiety were overwhelming that night. I cried off-and-on until about 2am, and then once I finally went to sleep, I was restless, waking up with a jolt every hour or so.

During one of those sleepless, delirious moments in the middle of the night, I promised myself that I would call in sick to work when morning came. I reconsidered once the sun came up, though. I certainly didn't feel like going to work, but the thought of being in the apartment seemed like a worse option—especially if Liam came by. I had no idea when he would be coming back, and I honestly didn't know if he would call or text to let me know beforehand.

Liam breaking up with me had come so out of nowhere that it was difficult for me to know which way was up. I knew that I should start doing practical things like deciding whether or not I would actually stay in the apartment by myself or move back to my parents' house. However, that would require telling my friends and family about the breakup, and that did not seem like a viable option yet. I could hardly even believe it myself, so telling someone else seemed impossible—wrong.

I thought that if I ignored it, maybe it would go away and my life would go back to the way it used to be. I imagined Liam coming back to me and us resuming our life like none of this ridiculous scenario had ever happened.

In some ways, that would be a relief. But really and truly, when it came down to it, I would never feel the same about him after he had been so detached and cold about breaking my heart and leaving me alone.

I spent the entire following day of school on auto-pilot. I tried my best to be a good teacher and engage with the children even though I was far from okay.

They could tell something was wrong with me. A few of my more talkative, attentive students asked me if I was feeling okay, but once I assured them I was, they dropped the subject.

I made it through the day, feeling relieved that it was Friday while at the same time dreading the weekend alone. I had plans to go out with Liam and some of our friends on Saturday—plans that would not come to pass. There were eight or ten of us who were planning on hanging out. Kate and Collin were among them, and they were the ones who Liam had mentioned staying with. They were my friends, too, and it hurt to think that they already knew what was going on. I wondered what all Liam had told them and who else knew.

My day was full of thoughts, recollections, and fears about the future. I was so completely out-of-it that I just laughed when I opened the door of the apartment that afternoon and saw that my couch was missing. It was Liam's couch. He had been in this apartment for a year before I ever moved in with him, so it was mostly furnished when I got here. I had been hanging out at his place the whole time. I knew it was technically his couch, but it felt like it was mine, too. I was shocked to come home after work and find it was already missing.

I dropped my things near the door and crossed to the kitchen feeling devastated. Liam had said he would get his things, but for some reason, I thought he was talking about his clothes and toothbrush and insignificant things like that—not the couch.

I sat on a barstool and spread my arms onto the cold countertop, resting the side of my face on the hard surface with my eyes closed. I was mad about the couch and it caused me to be emotional and text Liam.

Me:
The couch is missing?!?

I attached a mad emoji and pressed send without any further thought.

I regretted it instantly.

I had a personal rule where I made myself wait fifteen minutes if I ever wanted to send a reactionary text, and I had broken it. When I sent it, I thought I was doing a good thing by writing so little since what I really wanted to do was say that *I'm moving out and threatening legal action if you don't help me settle with the landlord since your name is on the lease.*

My phone dinged seconds later, and I stared at the words on the screen.

Liam:
Did you not get the letter in the bedroom?!?

A letter.

There was a letter in the bedroom.

I stood and began walking that way immediately. I dreaded finding a letter, and at the same time I couldn't get to it fast enough. I actually considered that the letter could contain an apology. Maybe Liam was begging for my forgiveness. Maybe he was asking me to take him back. But then I realized that couldn't possibly be the case since the couch was already missing.

It was probably a letter trying to explain his behavior and telling me why he already moved the couch.

I blinked, feeling stupefied when I rounded the corner and stared into the bedroom.

Indeed, there was a folded piece of paper waiting for me on the floor.

It was where the bed used to be.

I didn't even spare the time to be dramatic about it I just shook my head in disbelief as I crossed to the middle of the floor and picked up the piece of paper.

My name was written on the front. Liam was an artist and everything he did had aesthetic appeal. My name was written in fancy block print. It was simple, but it was neat and beautiful and looked like Walt Disney could have written it.

I opened it and read the note inside.

Stella,

I'm sorry about taking the couch and bed without more notice. I mentioned it at the studio this morning, and Raegan's friend wanted it and had cash on hand. As I write this, I realize that I probably should have given you first dibs if you wanted to buy them first, but they were already sold by the time I thought about it. She gave me more than I thought I could get for them, and I need all the cash I can get for my move. I am so thankful for your understanding. Parting ways is heartbreaking for me, and I'm eternally grateful that you are so selfless and drama free. You will always have a special place in my heart, Stella.

All my love,
Liam

PS: Also, I will be selling my other furniture. I took pictures of it to post. If you're interested in any of it, let me know soon. I will make you a good deal.

(He drew a little cartoon of a guy smiling and winking at the bottom of the page.)

I was so enraged that I felt nauseated.

I stared at the paper. There was a line that said *all my love*, and then there was a cartoon of a guy winking cheesily and a line that said he would make me a deal on what I thought was already my furniture.

I flopped on the floor where the bed used to be. I sat cross-legged for a second, but then I went ahead and stretched out on my back, staring at the ceiling and wondering how my life had been completely turned upside-down in the last twenty-four hours.

I couldn't just let him do this to me.

I didn't have to be understanding just because he thanked me in a note for not causing drama. It was my right to cause drama in this situation.

It wasn't that I wanted to cause drama, he had already done that. He was the one who had caused the drama. All I wanted to do was move out. I was not about to get stuck with nine months in an empty apartment. I didn't want to be there without him, anyway. To me, the apartment was worth $700 and not $1400. I couldn't fathom that he just expected me to take over paying for it with no objections.

I was utterly astounded that the same guy I had been with for almost two years could be so heartless and cold. It was like I was dealing with two different people. I wondered about his true intentions and thought maybe he had something romantic going on with that girl at the gallery.

Thoughts like that only made me angry, though. They didn't do me any good. It didn't matter what drove him to do it, anyway. There was no use torturing myself with speculation.

It was just that it was humiliating—thinking of telling everyone what had happened. That aspect of it made me want to stay in the apartment. I hated the idea of moving back into my parents' house after being away for only three months.

When Liam and I first got together, he had been the one to pursue me. It was just a fact that Liam was the one who started liking me before I even noticed him. I had been reluctant about getting into a relationship, but he didn't give up. He actively wooed me with poetry and art and his talent and quick wit.

I loved Liam, and I thought he was equally in love with me—if not more. I just always thought I had the upper hand in our relationship, and not in a full-of-myself type of way. That was just the dynamic we had in the past. Liam was definitely the one who came after me. That was what made this all the more shocking and embarrassing.

I started to text Liam back right away, but instead I stayed there, staring at the ceiling. I stared to one side and then the other, to stretch my neck. Liam hadn't even bothered sweeping the floor where the bed had been. There was dust and hair a few other random things like a balled-up tissue and a ponytail holder or two. It was kind of gross, but I didn't care at all. I didn't even care that I was lying on a hard floor.

I stared at the ceiling again and then stayed there for what must have been an hour—thinking about everything.

Then I called my mother.

That was difficult for me to do.

My mother had cried when I told her I was moving in with Liam in the first place. He and I had been dating for a long time, so it wasn't like I rushed into it, but she and my father were still disappointed in me for choosing to do that. Mom didn't make a big show of it or act like it was the end of the world, but she had shed a few tears when I told her. She and my dad were old school that way. They thought that us living together meant we weren't doing "things the right way". She and my father were go-to-church-every-Sunday type of people.

I loved God and everything, but I didn't see any need to go to church every time the doors opened. I had talked to Liam about it, and we had basically come to the conclusion that we would be Easter and Christmas church-goers. Liam just went along with what I wanted, actually. He wasn't raised going to church and he didn't think it was as important as I did. He basically wanted to appease me and just agreed with whatever I said on the subject. I wasn't opposed to going, but I hadn't been in months—not since before I moved into the apartment.

All this to say, I knew that telling my mom about the break up would give her every right to say she told me so about it being a bad idea in the first place.

I called her, and I began crying the instant I started telling her about it.

Within twenty minutes, my mother was at my apartment.

I opened the door, and she was standing there smiling lovingly but regretfully at me. She stepped into the apartment, closing the door before crossing immediately to me. She took me into her arms and I went willingly. I felt no judgement or disappointment—only love and tenderness.

"I'm so sorry," she said, rubbing my back and not even mentioning the missing couch. I had told her about it on the phone, anyway. "Everything's going to be all right," she continued. "I know it doesn't feel like it right now, but it will. I promise. We're going to work it out with Liam and your landlord. Things like this happen, baby. It's probably not the first time your landlord has had to deal with someone breaking their lease. It's not going to be a big deal logistically at all. Dad and your brothers will bring the truck over here and you can move back in with us for a little while until you get it figured out."

We stayed there for a minute in silence.

Mom just held me there.

"Okay?" she asked finally, making sure I heard her.

I nodded, still resting my head on her shoulder.

She rubbed my back again. "It's all going to be okay," she said.

I nodded again, though at the moment I didn't feel so sure.

Chapter 3

Roughly six weeks later

I didn't have time to slow down and lick my wounds after everything that happened with Liam, and it was probably better that way. Moving back to my parents' house wasn't as big of a deal as I anticipated, but I threw myself into my work, and before I knew it, we were approaching the end of November.

It was the Tuesday before Thanksgiving, so I was currently on break from school. By tradition, our whole family celebrated Thanksgiving at our house. It was always a large group, and my mom was already at work buying groceries, preparing the menu, and adding last-minute fall touches to the house. She wasn't much of a chef, but there were a few basic casseroles that she had perfected over the years, and other members of the family brought over their own contributions. My dad and Uncle Ezekiel were in charge of frying a turkey.

Mom had a friend over and they were decorating the living room when I came out of my bedroom that morning. It was 11am, but I was still in my pajamas, so it didn't surprise me when my mom asked if I had just woken up.

"No ma'am," I said. "I've been up since eight, catching up on some lesson planning. Hey, Mrs. Ellis."

I added that last part when I made eye contact with my mother's friend, Mrs. Ellis, who was sitting there, keeping my mother company while she decorated the house.

"I can't believe you've been up since eight o'clock and you haven't come out here for breakfast or coffee yet," Joni Ellis said, taking a sip from her own mug as if to indicate the importance of coffee.

Her eyes were wide, and I smiled at her. "I ate a protein bar in my room," I said.

"And she's got a coffee pot in there, too," my mom added.

I nodded since I had been about to say that myself. I crossed to the kitchen where I opened the fridge and then poured myself a glass of orange juice.

"Ross said he saw you last week at the movie theater," Joni said.

I smiled and nodded, knowing she would bring that up. I had seen her husband the weekend before. It was crowded on a Saturday night, so we didn't talk, but I saw him and waved at him.

"He and Allen Ridgefield went to see that new superhero movie," she said. "You'd think they were fifteen."

"Oh, no, all my boys love those movies," Mom said. "Even Ricky and my dad go see them. I don't think guys ever grow out of that."

"I like 'em too," I said, after I swallowed a sip of juice.

"Yeah, Isabel does too," Joni said, nodding and talking about her daughter. "Is that what you were seeing?" she asked me.

"No ma'am. I saw that one with Logan Ritchie."

"Oh, I heard that was good," she said.

I nodded. "It was."

"Did you go with a *young man*?" she asked. She smiled and made a mischievous face, raising her eyebrows. She was one of my mom's good friends, therefore she knew about my break up with Liam. Going out with a guy was so totally the last thing on my mind that I let out a little laugh as I answered.

"No ma'am," I said. "I went with a few of my friends from work. Girls."

"Oh, I thought maybe there was a new gentleman in your life." she said.

"Noooo," I said in a silly but certain tone. "Not for at least a few years. Maybe never."

"Oh, now, surely you don't mean that, Stella Claire."

That comment came from my mother, and I gave her a questioning glance, wondering why she would seem surprised. I assumed it was reasonable that anyone who had been through what I had would swear off men.

"She'll meet somebody," Mom said.

"Oh, I know she will," Joni assured her.

I just smiled and drank the last bit of my juice, resisting the urge to tell them they didn't know what they were talking about. I wasn't trying to be cynical about it, but I was honestly in no hurry whatsoever to meet a man. For the time being, I didn't even notice men in public or check them out.

"I'm going to the gym," I said, changing the subject.

"Oh, that's over by the church," Mom said. "Could you take a casserole by there for me?"

"Ross and I sent a plant," Joni said. "I would have sent a casserole, but I wasn't sure with Thanksgiving coming."

"I talked to Catherine and told her I would make that hashbrown casserole since it was Tim's favorite. I bought a ham, too. She's got a house full right now. Tim's sister and her family are staying with them and Caleb's back in town, you know. I think he's got a place, but I'm sure he goes over there to eat."

I had no idea what they were talking about, honestly. I did recognize the names Tim and Catherine, though. Tim Gray was the pastor at the church where my parents had been going since I was a small child. It was a huge church, but my parents knew everyone including the pastor and his wife. I had never gotten to know as many people as they did. Even when I was forced to go there every week, I just hung out with the people I already knew from school and left when the service was over. But I did recognize their names when she said them.

"So, would you mind taking that casserole by the church?" Mom asked, looking at me.

"And a ham?"

"Yes. And a ham. I told Catherine I'd drop it by sometime before three."

"What's it for?" I asked, not wanting to awkwardly walk into a church event with my gym clothes on.

"Tim's mom passed away last week," Mom said. "Miss Lucille."

The name Miss Lucille didn't really ring any bells, but I nodded and gave them a sad smile to reflect my regret about her passing.

"She was in her nineties," Joni said. "She didn't have Tim till she was older."

"Is the funeral going on?" I asked. "I wouldn't even know where to drop it off."

"Oh, no, they already had it on Saturday," Mom said. "Catherine just asked me to wait a day or two since they had so much food last weekend."

"It's like the practice run for your Thanksgiving dinner," Joni said.

"I'm not making hashbrown casserole Thursday," Mom said. "Ricky likes Rhonda's mashed potatoes, so she's bringing those."

"So, do I just drop them off somewhere?" I asked, getting back to the point so I could go back to my room to get dressed.

"Yes," Mom said. "Just take them to the church office and tell whoever is at the front desk that you need to leave them in the fridge for the Gray family. They'll know what it's about. Catherine is going by there this afternoon to pick it up."

"Yeah, but she better not take it in through the gym," Joni said. "They're hosting that Thanksgiving thing for homeless people."

"Oh, that's right," Mom said, looking at me. "You know where the offices are, right? The gym is on the complete opposite side. Don't go into the gym, because it will get lost in the shuffle with all that food."

"It's fine, I'll find it," I said.

I was just happy that all I had to do was drop it off. I wasn't completely sure where the offices were, but I had been in the church gym before, and I knew I would be able to ask someone for directions if I got confused.

"Thank you," Mom said. "That's one less thing I have to do today."

While I was getting dressed, she packaged the casserole and ham in a large thermal bag. Both of them were cold, and she included a note with heating instructions.

"It's heavy," Mom said when I looked inside the bag a few minutes later. "Sorry about that. I put a sympathy card in there as well. It's on top."

I closed the bag and lifted upward on the handles, testing the weight of it. It was heavy, but nothing I couldn't lift.

"Speaking of church," Mom said, "I thought you'd want to come with us this Sunday. Little Sophie's getting baptized."

"Sophie Wilde?" I asked, referring to my first cousin on my dad's side.

Mom nodded. My dad's brother had three daughters and Sophie was the youngest. She was twelve, and for the last two years, I had been giving her piano lessons.

"Aunt Becky called me yesterday to let me know. Isn't that sweet? She's doing it at the eleven o'clock service. I know she'd love it if you came."

I nodded. "Okay," I said noncommittally.

"Okay, you'll come?" Mom asked.

I glanced at Joni Ellis who was sitting there listening to our conversation.

"Sure," I said. "I'll go."

"Aw, good," Mom said excitedly. "That's great. It's this Sunday."

I nodded.

"And thank you for taking this by the church."

***

I pulled into the parking lot a little while later, staring at the vast expanse of buildings and wondering which door led to the offices. I knew where the gym was, so I drove to the opposite end of the campus and parked in a spot near some random doors that looked like they might perhaps lead to the place I needed to go. I retrieved the heavy bag from the back seat of my car and headed toward the doors with it.

There was construction going on nearby. A few gentlemen were working. I could see that they had part of the roof off but I didn't stop to check out what they were doing since they were a ways off.

I was about ten or fifteen feet from the door when I noticed that one of them was headed toward me. He was a young man.

Not that I was looking, but it was impossible not to notice that he was nice-looking, handsome (as far as brutish construction workers went). He literally had on a tool belt. He looked like one of those TV guys who would have his own home improvement show. I glanced over his shoulder at the thought to make sure there was no camera following him.

"Let me get that for you," he said as he approached. He motioned toward the bag that I was carrying.

"Oh, no, that's okay. I've got it."

"Are you sure?" he asked.

I nodded and he doubled back taking a few steps toward the door since he could see that was where I was headed. He opened it for me. He was definitely there with the construction crew, so I was almost certain that he couldn't help me find my way, but I asked anyway since he was standing there and available.

"Do you happen to know if this is the entrance for the church offices?" I asked as I walked past him into the door. "I'm not even sure if I'm in the right place. I have some food to drop off."

"The offices are that way," he said, pointing down the hallway toward our left. "But I can take it for you. I'd be happy to do that. Does it need to go in the refrigerator? I assume it does, with the bag."

"It does go in the fridge, but it's not for the Thanksgiving thing. That's something different. I need to make sure it gets to the right place. Thank you, though."

I gave the gentleman a nod like I expected us to part ways while I sought out the offices.

"If you tell me who it belongs to, I can make sure they get it," he said.

I stared up at him. He was a sizeable guy. I came from a basketball family, so I was used to tall men, but this guy was big. He was thick and muscular. He was not my type at all, but he was the definition of a handsome man—a clean-cut, hard-working slice of all-American wholesome handsomeness. There were no tattoos or piercings like Liam—just a ruggedly handsome face with a perfect jawline dusted with facial hair, and a row of shiny white teeth. He was probably the quarterback of his high school football team. He seemed like the take-charge type, too. He probably owned the construction business that the church had hired. Any other girl would have been taken.

"This is actually for the pastor of the church," I said, ignoring his appearance. "My mom asked me to bring it up here. They had a death in the family."

"Oh, that was so nice of you," he said. "Tell Miss Sara thanks for doing that."

I tilted my head curiously at him when he said my mother's name, and he smiled the instant he noticed my confusion. "You don't remember me," he said. It was a statement and not a question. "I'm Tim and Catherine's oldest son, Caleb."

I knew the pastor and his wife had two boys, but I didn't know either of them. I vaguely remembered them, but one of them was a little older than me and the other was younger, so I had never gotten to know either of them.

"Oh, okay," I said, nodding like I remembered even though I didn't. I definitely didn't remember either of them looking like this guy. "I'm sorry about that. I thought you were just working here. Was it your grandma that passed away?"

"It was," he said.

"I'm sorry to hear that."

His mouth turned upward in a regretful smile. "Thank you. Tell your mom I said this food won't go to waste."

"I think your mom is supposed to pick it up this afternoon," I said. "She talked to my mom who told me that I needed to avoid giving it to the people in the gym who were doing the Thanksgiving dinner.

That's all I know. I'm sure you can help me make sure your mom gets it."

"We'll put it back here in the fridge," he said, motioning down the hall and looking at me like he wanted me to follow him. He reached out for the bag again, and this time I handed it to him. He took it from me holding it up without flinching like it weighed less than a pound. I had been struggling with it and I smiled at how effortlessly he carried it.

"Did you move away or something?" I asked, trying to remember him. He looked so completely different from the boy I remembered as Tim Gray's son that I had to ask.

"I did," he said. "I went to seminary over in London, and I've lived there since."

"London, England?" I asked. I felt silly for saying that, and I let out a little laugh. "I guess it wouldn't be London, Kentucky."

Caleb smiled. "My mother would have loved it if that was the case. But, yes, I was in England."

"Wow," I said, glancing at him and nodding as we walked. He had a plaid shirt under his khaki jacket. His pants, although well-fitted and flattering, were working-man pants, plain as day. He had on work boots as well. I saw them because I glanced downward as we walked. "Do you still live there?" I asked. "London. Do you live there still?" I thought maybe he was just home for the funeral, or Thanksgiving or both.

"I just moved back," he said. "Last week."

"How long were you there?" I asked.

"Seven years."

"Gosh, that's a long time," I said, nodding and thinking it was no wonder I didn't recognize him. He had left looking like a kid and came back a man. I glanced at his profile, at the short patches of hair that grew on his jaw, and I appreciated how very masculine he was.

"I should... I guess... if you're carrying the bag... there's really no reason for me to follow you in there," I said.

I didn't think the statement was going to come across as awkward, but a sudden wave of nerves came over me as I was talking. "I know you need to get back to what you were doing, and I don't want to hold you up." I stopped in the middle of the hall to turn around and head out the way I came in. Caleb stopped and looked straight at me. His dark brown eyes staring straight into mine. I reminded myself that this was not the type of guy I was normally attracted to, but it did no good. He was attractive. Period.

"What about your bag?" he asked.

"Oh, no, that's okay," I said, suddenly feeling like I couldn't get out of there fast enough. "You can just give it back when you give back the dish or whatever. Our moms will work it out."

"Are you sure?"

"Oh yeah, no, take it. My mom doesn't really care. She probably has like three of those."

There was just no way I should be checking out the manliness of this straight-laced carpenter who went to seminary. I made my exit in a hurry.

"Well, it was nice seeing you, Stella. Thanks for the food."

"Oh, you're welcome. No problem."

He had said my name, but I hadn't told it to him. He remembered me. I waved and smiled at him as I retreated, but I was already halfway to the door.

Chapter 4

The next few days were full.

High school and college basketball season was just getting started, which was a big deal for our family. My little brother, Tanner, was in his senior year in high school and was a stand-out MVP type. Jordan, my first cousin on my mother's side, played college ball for the University of Kentucky.

My mother's brother, Uncle Ezekiel (or Uncle E as we called him), was an extremely successful basketball player who played both college and pro ball before retiring from the sport to run a horse farm right here in Lexington. Uncle E was one of the most legendary American athletes and now he was tearing it up in the world of horse breeding and racing—he was just one of those people who everything he touched turned to gold.

My cousin, Jordan, seemed to be taking after him in that way. He was in his senior year at UK, and he was one of the most popular and dynamic players on the team. It didn't hurt that he was Ezekiel Tanner's son, but Jordan was a good player, and he was making a name for himself. He wasn't sure about playing pro, but with the way his senior year was going, it seemed like a possibility.

Jordan had a home basketball game the Wednesday before Thanksgiving and my brother had one the Saturday afterward, and we all went to both of them. Between that and the Thanksgiving commotion, the end of my week shaped up to be really busy. I was glad that I had finished all of my grading and prep work for school earlier in the week.

Sunday morning came before I knew it. The following day, I would be going back to school for the first time after a week off.

I went out with some work friends Saturday night to celebrate/commiserate, and I woke up at 9am to my mother shaking my shoulder. I normally didn't sleep so late, but I had been hanging out at my friend Kami's house until two o'clock in the morning. I blinked at my mother through squinted eyes.

"What's up?" I asked groggily.

"We're leaving," she said. "Dad and I volunteer at the early service. I didn't know if you remembered to set an alarm or if you wanted me to wake you."

"For what?" I asked.

"Church."

I had been sleeping hard, and it took me a few seconds.

Church.

Sophie was getting baptized. I had completely forgotten that I told my mother I would go to that. I thought about the church and my sweet cousin, and then the next thing to cross my mind was Caleb Gray, the preacher's son. I remembered our chance meeting and thought about him living in London. I remembered he had said something about going to seminary there, but I wasn't sure. I thought he was a carpenter, but maybe he was a preacher. Thinking about him made me picture his face and I cringed at myself for doing it.

"What's the matter?" Mom asked.

"Nothing, I'm just waking up," I said, making sure my expression was neutral. "What time does it start?"

"Eleven. It's the late service. And they do the baptisms at the beginning."

I looked at the clock. It was barely nine o'clock, and I nodded and closed my eyes again.

"Do you want me to set your alarm for ten?" she asked.

"No, thank you," I said sleepily. "I'm up. I'm just closing my eyes for a minute."

"Tanner's going to the eleven o'clock service, too," Mom said. "You two should ride together. Dad's waking him up right now, but he might go back to sleep. You might want to check on him in an hour or so."

I nodded, eyes still closed.

"Are you getting up?" she asked.

I nodded again.

"Thank you," she said, patting my leg.

My mouth stretched into a slow smile. "Thanks for waking me up," I said.

"Okay. We'll see you there."

I never slept past nine o'clock anymore, but I had been up late the night before, and I was groggy. In spite of that, I shifted and got out of bed right when my mom left the room. Caleb crossed my mind again, and the thought of seeing him made me pop out of bed. I didn't think I was attracted to him, but I also didn't want to run into him in my gym clothes again. I had a little breakfast, drank some coffee, and then I put some effort into my appearance.

I pulled my dark hair into a loose twist and secured it with pins. It was a style I used all the time so knew just how much hair to pull down around the fringe and how much spray to use. It was my go-to easy-but-fancy style. It was cold out so I wore a light pink sweater with dark skinny jeans and a long wool coat.

My little brother and I went together. It was 10:15 when I went into his room to wake him up, and I basically had to peel him out of bed. He was a busy and popular high school senior, and I didn't even want to know what kind of trouble he was getting into on the weekends.

I rode with Tanner since he loved his truck and wanted to drive. We pulled into the parking lot with two minutes to spare. I knew we were cutting it close with making it there before they began singing, but hopefully we wouldn't miss Sophie's baptism. Tanner followed behind me as we headed through the parking lot.

"Why are you in such a hurry?" he asked as we made it to the main doors.

"You don't think we'll miss Sophie, do you?" I asked. "They used to do it after the songs, but I'm not sure how they do it now. I hope we don't miss it.

"Miss what?"

It was a man's voice.

It was Caleb.

He was the very first person I saw when the door swung open. He had been the one to open it for us. He was not dressed in carpenter's clothes. He was in slacks and a button-down shirt, looking formal and dashing. His style was still nowhere near as fashion-forward as Liam's, but he wasn't dressed in work clothes. We were the only ones coming through the door at the moment, so Caleb let the doors close behind us.

"I was hoping we didn't miss Sophie's baptism," I said, once we made it inside.

"You didn't," Caleb promised, smiling at me confidently like he knew just what I was talking about. "Good morning Wilde family," he continued with a small bow. He shook Tanner's hand before turning to me. "Where are your ear muffs?" he asked. He grinned at me, and before I knew what was happening, his warm hands came up and gently rested around my ears in makeshift earmuffs. His hands were big and warm, and my ears were seriously freezing.

The contact felt entirely too good.

I watched his expression change.

He was joking and smiling with me about coming in without my ears covered, but I saw his smile fade just before he took his hands off of me. It happened quickly. It was like he suddenly realized that he felt a certain way about touching me. Or maybe he realized that I felt a certain way about him touching me.

The thought caused me to blush.

"It's really great to see you guys," he said. "Thank you for coming this morning. Enjoy the service."

He wasn't trying to shoo us away, but someone else was coming up to the door, and he had to hold it open it for them. I was listening to him greet the next group as I walked away.

Tanner and I headed to the next set of doors that led into the sanctuary. The whole interaction with Caleb had only lasted a few seconds, but my heart was left pounding. I laughed nervously at the memory of his earmuff remark. Maybe he wasn't as affected as I was. I really had no idea what he was thinking when his smile faded. It bothered me that I even cared what he was thinking.

Someone was waiting at the next set of doors, offering us a church bulletin. We took it and walked into the main auditorium. They had just started singing, and I followed Tanner because he knew right where our parents were sitting. I thought about Caleb touching my face and the way his expression changed as he pulled his hands off of me. I tried not to think about him or feel attracted to him, but I couldn't help it. He was pure and genuine and I instantly felt a sense of comfort around him.

Tanner and I found our parents and I stood next to them while musicians performed three songs. I sat next to my mother who sang every note to every song and didn't miss a lyric even though her eyes were closed and she couldn't see the screens. There was a time when I knew the songs they sang by heart, but these were new to me. Thankfully, the lyrics were displayed on the screen.

Three people were baptized that morning, and Sophie was the final one to go. I wasn't expecting to react emotionally to it, but I cried when I watched her. The pastor asked Sophie if she had accepted Christ into her heart, and when she answered with, "Yes sir," I had to look away to keep from having my face completely crumple with tears.

The pastor said a prayer after Sophie's baptism and then he made his way to the middle of the stage, talking as he walked. He dried his hands and arms with a towel, and then he handed it to someone who had come on stage specifically to take it. They had a huge congregation, and they ran their service smoothly.

"It's always such an honor to be able to see someone take that next step in baptism," Tim Gray said, smiling as he approached the center of the stage. "We had two of them in our early service, and I tell you, it makes for a great morning." (He paused while people clapped.) "It's an extra special morning for me because I get to introduce you to our guest speaker who happens to be one of my favorite people in the whole world."

Caleb walked onto the stage, smiling and waving when the crowd clapped. "You might have seen this handsome young man standing at the door when you came in," Tim said as Caleb joined him at center stage. Everyone clapped and made various noises of approval.

My mom leaned over to speak near my ear. "That's his son," she informed me.

I nodded.

"He just moved back to town," she added, staring at the stage but talking to me.

"Our son, Caleb, left Kentucky seven long years ago," Tim said nostalgically. "We always imagined he'd grow up and go to college right here at the University of Kentucky like any good red-blooded American would..." (He smiled and paused briefly while everyone laughed.) "But the Lord had other plans for Caleb. He decided to go to seminary in London, England, of all places." (He stared at Caleb thoughtfully, and then smiled at the crowd.) "Let me back up and say that when he left for the UK, he was five-foot-six-inches tall. Some of you remember him that way. Some of you probably haven't seen him since then and you were wondering who this new guy was standing at the door. Anyway, in the first year after he moved, he grew seven inches. Seven inches in one year. And not until he was eighteen. Can you imagine that? We didn't even know that was possible. We wondered what he was eating over there in London and when he would stop growing." (He paused while people laughed and reacted.) "But the Lord grew Caleb in stature and in wisdom, y'all. He got plugged-in in London, and ended up staying there long after he graduated. Catherine and I thought he might get married and have our grandbabies over there. If that was the case, I'd be giving a whole different speech right now—one where I'm telling you the rest of us are packing up and moving to Europe." (He paused again while people laughed.)

Tim Gray was a captivating speaker who had everyone engaged, but I still felt nervous for Caleb who was standing there next to his father with literally every eye on them. *Had Tim said that Caleb was going to be a guest speaker?* I reminded myself that it was silly for me to feel nervous for him either way. There was no reason for me to have any feelings at all on the subject. *He had gone to England for seven years. It was interesting. And he was a handsome guy. So what?*

I stuck to staring blankly at the stage. Tim wasn't a small man. He and Caleb were about the same height and both of them were broad-chested. They stood side-by-side with Tim's hand resting on Caleb's back. Caleb smiled as his father spoke.

"But no, in all seriousness, Catherine and I are extremely proud of Caleb and the work God has done in and through him these last seven years over in England. While he was studying at seminary, he worked as a carpenter's apprentice. So, Caleb's not only a pastor, but he also does some outstanding carpentry work. He's a true craftsman. Needless to say, Caleb was a busy guy over there. He was in leadership at a church and also working as a carpenter when his mother and I called him up and said something completely unexpected. What'd we say?" Tim asked, turning to look at Caleb.

"You said you wanted to hire me as the new associate pastor here at your church."

"We did, we sure did say that," Tim said, delivering it and nodding in just the right way that it caused people to laugh. "And what was your answer?"

"I said I'd love to," Caleb said, smiling.

A picture of Caleb came up on the jumbo screens. It was a gorgeous, professionally taken photograph of him with his name and the title *associate pastor* written underneath it.

The crowd clapped and cheered when it came onto the screen, and it caused Caleb and Tim to smile and look behind them to see what we were seeing.

"He took a week to think and pray about it first," Tim said teasingly before looking at Caleb with a sincere expression. Again, he patted his son's back.

"We are absolutely thrilled to welcome him to our staff, you guys, and it's not just because he's our son or because he can swing a hammer." (Laughter.) "No, the most important thing is that Caleb is a young warrior for Christ. He's an excellent teacher and he's got a heart for the Lord. You'll see what I mean in just a minute as he brings the Word. So, it's without further ado that I introduce you to your new associate pastor, Caleb Gray."

Everyone erupted in applause, and I clapped right along with them.

Chapter 5

Caleb Gray talked about God in a down-to-earth way that rang true to my heart.

He was young, smart, and funny, and he seemed to know God so intimately that it was easy for him to introduce me to Him. I could have easily fallen for Caleb, but honestly, after listening to him talk, it was Jesus I had fallen for.

Caleb painted a picture of Jesus our Savior, the great and mighty King who was all-powerful and yet accessible.

Something changed inside of me as I listened to Caleb's words. He made it seem like giving Christ lordship of my life was the best choice I could make—the only logical choice. I sat there listening and feeling convicted and stirred, changed. I had grown up hearing the gospel and believing it, but I had spent my life being focused on other things.

Caleb's words caused my thinking to shift. I felt like I had a different perspective on the things of eternity, and I didn't want to waste any more of my time on this earth ignoring it.

In a moment of doubt, I wondered if I was more receptive to what Caleb was saying because he was so dynamic on stage and good looking. But it wasn't about Caleb or what he personally brought to the table. It was more than that. It wasn't the person saying it, but what was being said.

He prayed a prayer at the end of the service, and I found myself praying it and meaning it.

***

"He's as good as his daddy," Mom said when the service ended and we were dismissed.

She was talking to my Aunt Rhonda who was sitting in front of us and had turned around when he finished. Tanner had already begun to head for the door, but I stayed to hear what Mom and Aunt Rhonda were going to say.

"I know," my aunt agreed, nodding. "He's so good. I remember him speaking last year when he came home for Christmas, and wow. Larry told E they were grooming him to take over for Tim when he retires."

My mom made a confused face.

"Not tomorrow or anything," Aunt Rhonda said. "Like ten or fifteen years down the road. With a congregation this size, you have to ease them into change."

Mom nodded as if it made sense. Neither of them looked at me for my opinion. They assumed I didn't care. The truth was that I was still reeling from all the thoughts and feelings I had regarding God and the message I had just heard. It was on my mind to the extent that I almost mentioned it. I contemplated saying something about how I really enjoyed what he had said, but I held it in.

We all began to walk toward the door as a group. Uncle Ezekiel was a celebrity and sometimes, if we didn't leave a public place right away, people would stop him to talk and it would take him an hour to get out of the building.

Mom stopped in her tracks. "Oh, Rick, I'll meet you at the truck. I forgot Catherine's got my dish." She looked at me. "I don't know where Tanner took off to. Did you ride up here with him?"

"Yes," I said, looking over my shoulder for my brother.

"He'll wait for you," Dad told me.

"I'll walk with Mom," I said. "If you see Tanner, tell him to go ahead and I'll just ride home with you guys."

"Yeah, he's right there talking to his friends," Uncle Ezekiel had heard our conversation and was tall enough to scout out my brother and report on his whereabouts.

"I'll tell him you're riding with Mom and me," Dad said.

"Tell precious Sophie we said congratulations." Aunt Rhonda made the statement as she reached out to hug my mom.

I wasn't sure where my mom had to go to get the dish, but we were parting ways with everyone else at this point. I said goodbye to my family who had been sitting with us—my aunt and uncle, and my cousin, Zeke, along with wife, Allison.

Within a minute, my mother and I were headed toward the stage instead of away from it. "Thanks for coming this morning," Mom said, glancing at me as we walked.

She put her arm through mine, and I smiled, feeling introspective and not really knowing how to respond. "I'm happy I came," I said.

"Are you okay?" Mom asked, focusing on me as we continued to walk.

I nodded thoughtfully. "I'm just tired," I said. "And I'm thinking about work tomorrow." It was a lie, and it was right on the heels of me feeling like I wanted to do better with my life, but I didn't know how to say what I was feeling. Besides, it wasn't a total lie. Work was definitely in the back of my mind. Tomorrow would be my first day back after a week off, so of course I was thinking about it. But other things were certainly on the forefront of my thoughts.

I contemplated everything as we moved closer to the front of the stage. There was a group of people standing there who had stayed behind to talk to the pastor and his family. Most of the congregation left, but enough people stayed behind that we had to wait our turn to speak with them.

"Oh, hey, Sara!" Catherine Gray said when we stepped up to them. "Hey there, Stella. How are you doing, sweetie?" She asked the question as she ushered us toward her left—away from her husband and Caleb. There was another guy standing there as well, and I assumed he was Caleb's little brother.

I walked away with my mom and Catherine even though I wanted to say something to Caleb about how much I enjoyed the service.

"I'm fine, how are you?" I said, answering Mrs. Gray's question as I followed them.

"We're doing good. So happy to have Caleb back. Your dish and bag are right over here," she added, explaining where we were going. "Thank y'all so much for the food. I didn't know you were going to send a ham. That was so thoughtful of you."

"I figured with boys in the house, and Tim's family..."

"Oh, it got eaten," Catherine said in an over-exaggerated tone that made my mother laugh.

I glanced over my shoulder as they continued to talk. Other people had approached Caleb, but he saw me turn. I was about to look away when his eyes caught mine. He smiled and waved at me. I hesitated for a second, but then I smiled and waved back.

I wanted to say something to him. I wanted to thank him and tell him that his words made a difference in my heart. He was busy, so I settled for a smile, but I made it as sincere as I could. Caleb had to turn and shake the hand of someone who had come up to him, but I secretly loved the fact that he seemed a little disappointed about breaking eye contact with me.

"Your son did an excellent job this morning," my mother said, speaking to Catherine.

"Thank you. We are so excited about having him back. He liked it over there. Tim and I thought he'd never come back home."

"Josiah's up there shaking hands with his dad and brother," Mom said. "Is he going to follow in their footsteps?"

"You mean become a pastor? No. Josiah has no interest in full-time ministry. He's studying art."

"Well, I knew he was going to UK, but I didn't know he was an artist." (Mom looked at me.) "Stella knows a lot of people over there in that department."

"Yes ma'am," Catherine said, smiling and nodding. "He wants to be an animator."

Artists were usually my type. As a musician, I myself was an artist. And, of course, there was Liam. I hadn't looked at Josiah other than to vaguely take in the fact that there was a young man standing next to Caleb who was probably his brother.

By that time, we had made it to the row of chairs where my mom's things were located and we stopped walking. I was curious about Josiah and I turned and looked over my shoulder again.

And.

Oh, goodness.

Caleb.

He wasn't thirty feet away, standing next to his dad and brother like I expected him to be. He was... heading... straight... toward... me.

"There he is!" my mom said, reaching out to hug him as he approached us. "Goodness, Caleb. I was

55

just telling your mom what a good job you did this morning."

"Oh, I really appreciate that," Caleb said, hugging her.

"We all enjoy it so much when you speak. My brother was saying that he wanted to talk to you about working with the basketball team some—you know, speaking to them."

"Yes ma'am, Mr. Tanner called me."

"Oh, he did? Good."

Caleb was wearing an easy smile as he seamlessly shifted his focus from my mother to me. "I was actually coming to see if you were coming tonight," he said.

I had no idea what he was talking about, but in that moment, I felt like I would agree to go just about anywhere. "Where?" I asked.

"To work on the Christmas boxes," he said.

He could see by my expression that I wasn't sure what he was talking about, and he continued, "We're doing it tonight and next Sunday. We meet in the student venue from five to seven to stuff those Christmas boxes. It's fun. We play Christmas music, and there's pizza and drinks."

I was just about to smile and ask if there would be hot chocolate, but before I could say anything, my mother spoke up.

"I was just talking to Stella about all she had to do to get ready for work tomorrow," Mom said, explaining, making an excuse for me. "She's a first-grade teacher and they've been off for Thanksgiving break. She goes back in the morning." Mom was trying to do me a favor. She knew church wasn't a regular thing for me and she didn't want the invitation to make me feel on the spot.

"What time did you say it was happening?" I asked, looking at Caleb.

"Five to seven," he said. "But I understand about going back to work. I just wanted to mention it to you."

"It was great seeing you," his mother said to my mother when she saw that someone was waiting to talk to her. "Thanks again for the food. Everything was wonderful."

"It was great, Mrs. Wilde," Caleb agreed. He touched his flat stomach. "I ate more than my share of it."

"Aw, thank you," Mom said, even though they were the ones thanking her.

"I think I'll come to that thing tonight," I said, speaking up before Caleb could walk away.

"Really?"

"Really?" Caleb and my mother said it at the exact same time.

Caleb was happy and curious, and my mom was genuinely surprised.

"Yeah, I think so," I said. "All I have to do is look over my stuff tonight. It's only like thirty minutes or an hour of work."

"Great," Caleb said, grinning as he began to walk away with his mom. "See you tonight Five o'clock. Student venue."

I waved and gave him a nod. "Yeah, see you then."

Chapter 6

"It's beginning to look a lot like Christmas..."

The lyrics to the classic song were the first thing I heard when I opened the door at the student venue. *"...Every where I go..."*

The song continued playing, but it became part of the background when my attention was drawn to the group standing by the door. It was a bunch of younger girls—high school aged. There were at least six of them standing in a group, and they all turned to look at me when I stepped inside.

I smiled at them and they didn't smile back. They weren't being outright rude, but they also didn't make an effort to welcome me. Most of them pretended like they hadn't seen me smile and went back to what they were doing huddled in a circle. Two of them were brave enough to keep staring at me, checking me out. But none of them smiled back—they just looked me over. Sure, they were just in high school and therefore were no competition to me at all—but the way they acted made me feel like they thought I was some kind of competition to them.

There were several other people there, though. I walked away from their obviously closed group, headed for anyone who could tell me where to go. (If I couldn't find that, maybe at least a smiling face.)

The Christmas music was playing, and the atmosphere seemed festive, but all I could see were people I didn't know who were already standing around in groups talking to each other.

I didn't know why I ever thought about going there alone. For some reason, I thought others would be there alone, too. But it wasn't like that. It was like a party—one where I didn't know anyone but they knew each other. I walked slowly so it wasn't obvious that I didn't know where I was going.

Those teenagers and their less than warm welcome reminded me why I didn't go to church. That cynical thought caused me to cringe. I felt changed in my heart after this morning, and that made me realize just how jaded I had been about church. I needed to make an effort to give them the benefit of the doubt. I couldn't let myself write off this whole experience because a couple of high-school girls looked at me funny.

Christmas music continued to play in the background, and the sound of it made me remember what I was there for. Packing boxes. I glanced around, taking in my surroundings and looking for something that had to do with checking in or getting to work. There were tables set up all along the back wall along with bags and bags of various items from different stores. I couldn't make sense of any of it, but I figured walking toward a table was the most logical choice.

"Well, hello, Miss Stella Wilde, how are you doing?" I turned to find a man standing there smiling at me. He was in his fifties or sixties. This gentleman had been coming to church here for a long time— since I was a little girl. I was relatively sure his name was Danny, but I wasn't sure enough to say it. He was a giant of a man, not just tall, but also big around, egg-shaped, like Humpty Dumpty. He held his arms out, inviting me to come in for a hug, so I did. I stepped toward him and put my arms around him. He was so large that my arms at full extension were only able to go about half-way around him. I patted his shoulders before stepping back.

"Do I need to go somewhere to... sign in or anything?" I asked, looking around tentatively.

"Oh, no, you mean to help out? No. Silvia's the one running it. She'll make an announcement in a minute and we'll get started."

The spot near the wall next to the man who I thought was named Danny seemed like as good a place as any for me to stand. I took a step back and positioned myself standing next to him. I looked out at the crowd, listening to *Holly Jolly Christmas* which had now begun playing.

I took in some faces, realizing that I knew more people than I thought. I recognized several groups of people in the room, but like the girls by the door, they were all consumed with their own conversations. I had expected a small group of ten or twelve people, but there were more like thirty or forty.

None of them were Caleb Gray.

I wondered if he was going to come.

In those seconds, while I was taking in my surroundings and wondering about Caleb, I heard someone else refer to the man next to me as Danny, so I knew I was correct about his name.

"How have you been doing?" Danny asked me after he spoke to that other person.

"Fine," I said. "I'm teaching now," I added, not knowing how much he knew about me.

"I thought your mom told me that," he said, nodding.

"What age?"

"First grade."

He chuckled knowingly, shaking his head, and I wondered if he knew how challenging it could be or if he was just being empathetic.

"What school?" he asked.

"L. Nelson Elementary."

"Oh, you probably know Peggy Gibson."

"I do. She's our principal."

"I know. She's a good friend of ours. I didn't know Sara and Ricky's daughter was working with Peggy. It's a small world. How do you like it over there?" He looked at me like he was prepared for me to say I didn't like it at all. "It's a challenging district. I know it's a calling for Peggy to be there."

"It's been a challenge," I agreed, trying to sound diplomatic. "I hope it's a calling for me to. I'm in my first year, so I still have to see how it goes. I didn't know I would have to be so thick-skinned for first-graders."

He laughed at that. "Unfortunately, you have to be thick-skinned for every age," he said.

We were still smiling from that comment when Caleb came in the door.

I watched from a distance as the girls who had been disinterested in my arrival broke into a run to get to the door and greet Caleb. There was a ruckus of voices and movement as they tripped all over themselves to go to the door and greet Caleb. That group of girls split apart and descended onto Caleb like moths to a flame. He might as well have been a celebrity.

"That's the pastor's son," Danny said. "Did you get to hear him speak this morning?"

"Yes sir," I said. "It was great. I really enjoyed it."

"Yeah, we're happy to have Caleb back in town."

"Everybody seems to be really excited about it," I said, referring to the mass of girls that fled to the door when he walked in.

"Those girls have been waiting by the door since four o'clock," Danny said, chuckling. "That's my granddaughter and her friends from the youth group. She came early with her Mimi. They all love Caleb and Josiah."

His granddaughter was one of the girls who had snubbed me when I walked in. I was glad I hadn't said anything to him about it.

"He's got every family in the church offering up their daughters and granddaughters on a silver platter," Danny said.

"Those girls are young for him," I said, a little too quickly.

Danny laughed. "Oh, I'm not offering *my* granddaughter," he said. "Not Isabel at least. Maybe Kara. But I wasn't talking about those girls. I'm just talking about the ladies in general. Caleb's such a gentleman. I guess that's hard to find nowadays. Silvia said he could be on a different blind date every night of the week if he wanted. All the church families just want to see their daughters end up with somebody good like him."

"I bet," I said stiffly.

"Miss Silvia's going to be getting everybody's attention here soon," Danny said, elbowing me and looking toward his wife. I glanced that way to see that she was indeed looking around like she was on the verge of getting everyone's attention. Danny whistled, causing me to jump and everyone to look our way. Danny gestured toward his wife who happily accepted the attention. She spoke loudly because the room was full and she didn't have a microphone.

She began by thanking everyone for coming, but I didn't hear much past that because I suddenly felt a hand on my arm. I turned to find Caleb standing beside me. He was dressed casually in jeans, a t-shirt, and a wind breaker. He had on running shoes and his dark hair was combed away from his face.

He was as put together as they come. I could see why the daughters were being offered to him. If I had a daughter his age, I'd offer her up, too. I smiled at the thought, and he smiled in response to me. He leaned in so that he could speak to me without interrupting Silvia. He kept his hand on my arm when he did that, and it caused me to hold my breath.

"I'm glad you made it," he said, near my ear. He was being innocent about it, but I noticed every little nuance about his proximity. He had a muscular, fit build. He was substantially bigger and broader than Liam, and the sheer size of him right next to me made me feel breathless.

"I'm glad I made it, too," I said, even though there were probably about a hundred other responses that would have been better than that. I was taken off-guard that he ended up right next to me so quickly considering the traffic jam at the door.

He took his hand off of my arm, but he didn't walk away. He stood right next to me, and that was where he stayed all evening.

He never left my side. He wasn't flirting with me, but it was as if he took a personal interest in making sure I was comfortable. He introduced me to people and made me feel like I was his guest. He talked to other people, but he always made sure I was included.

Caleb and I stuck by Danny all night. There were six or eight tables all set up to serve the same function. The three of us took over one end of a table with me between the two gentlemen. They talked to each other at first, and I enjoyed hearing their friendly banter.

Caleb was a people person, that was for sure. I watched him interact with everyone there, always being mindful of me and my comfort. He was a true gentleman—someone who seemed steeped in the ways of gentlemanly behavior. I wondered why I didn't remember him from when we were younger. I must have been focused on other things to the point that I completely missed seeing him and his potential.

Despite having plenty of opportunity, Caleb never touched me again after that initial contact with my arm. We talked to each other all evening, but our interactions were void of flirtatious behavior. Caleb looked me in the eyes—not checking me out at all. He asked me questions about my life and it didn't seem like he had any motives other than being nice and getting to know more about me.

I was surprised by how much one-on-one time we got, so I hadn't been prepared or given any thought to how I would behave in front of him. I answered all of his questions honestly and just acted like myself. As the middle child with two brothers, I was comfortable around men. Things were natural and easy between Caleb, Danny, and me.

We worked for over an hour, sorting toys and assembling boxes while listening to Christmas music. We laughed and had fun, and I actually felt good about the work we were doing. It occurred to me that I was the envy of every girl there, but I was just happy to find people who were friendly with me and seemed to want me there.

Chapter 7

Caleb Gray

Stella Wilde.

It was the third time Caleb had seen her recently, and he couldn't shake a certain feeling.

Caleb was close to God.

He was a man who lived his life constantly stepping out on faith and constantly having God catch him, protect him, and reward him for doing so. Caleb had the feeling in his heart that he would find his mate, his life partner, his wife when he moved back home to Kentucky. God had made that clear to him on multiple occasions, and since God showed up and showed how mighty He was in so many other aspects of his life, Caleb knew better than to doubt.

He fully expected to meet the woman of his dreams when he moved back home, and from the moment he laid eyes on Stella Wilde, he was convinced she was the one.

She was like a gift.

Physically, she was everything he desired.

He had never looked at Stella that way when he lived in Lexington years ago. He knew her a little back then, but he wasn't in the same frame of mind. He didn't realize until he laid eyes on her last week that she was exactly his type.

Everything about her seemed like God had designed her specifically for Caleb. In that way, she was almost supernatural looking to him. Maybe she was just supernatural looking, anyway. Her eyes were this impossibly bright green that shone like precious stones against her dark lashes and hair. She had some freckles across her nose, and her lips were a little too thin, and those things gave her face such a unique appearance. Caleb could not stop looking at her. She was an absolute work of art—the most beautiful thing he had ever seen. He was so attracted to Stella Wilde that he would probably suffer a little disappointment if she wasn't the woman God had chosen for him.

But, of course, she was.

He knew it in his bones.

He asked his mom about her last week when she brought the casserole to the church. The Wilde family was tied-in at the church, and everyone knew that Stella had been through a recent break up and that she never came to church anymore. Even this didn't dissuade him. He felt in his heart that he had seen the one who had been promised to him. It was as if a chapter in his life closed the minute he looked at her. He had never seen anyone else like he saw Stella.

Just that morning, he was standing at the door of the church, wishing, praying, and hoping that Stella would come. His mother had told him she didn't go to church anymore, but he still wished for it. He prayed for her to walk in. And there she was, in the nick of time, among the last guests for the last service.

In a moment of playfulness, Caleb placed his hands on her head, and his fingers felt like he had been shocked—alive with electricity. She sat with her family in the congregation. He could see them from the stage, and never did his feelings falter. He knew she was the one. Her family already felt like his family. Ezekiel Tanner was her uncle and was sitting in the row in front of her. He was Stella's mother's brother. Sure, Ezekiel was famous, and it would be great to marry into the Tanner family, but honestly that had nothing to do with his feelings. It was all Stella. She was his prize. She was the one.

Caleb was ecstatic when he came to the box-stuffing party to find that Stella had shown up. She had on black jeans and a fitted denim jacket. She had changed since church that morning, and she looked like a rebel with her glowing green eyes and black hair hanging over her shoulders. She was a little vixen. She looked intimidating and untamable on the outside, but her smile was genuine and her heart was soft and sweet.

He asked questions about her life and work, and Stella answered them with honesty that was refreshing. A couple of times, she mentioned playing piano. Caleb didn't know anything about her skill level, but he already knew this would only add to his attraction. He loved music. He didn't play an instrument, but he had always loved to watch and listen to others do it. He was smitten with Stella already, and it only made matters worse to hear her talk about playing piano.

"I'd love to hear you play sometime," Caleb said to her toward the end of the night. "Piano," he clarified since they hadn't been talking about piano when he mentioned it. Everyone was sitting around eating pizza at the end of the night, and Caleb made the statement seemingly out of nowhere.

"Oh, I, uh, I haven't... I graduated in May, and since then I haven't really performed much. In school, I played as an accompanist and in a jazz ensemble, but I've been so busy with teaching and giving lessons that I don't—"

"I meant I just want to hear you play sometime," he said, cutting her off. "It doesn't have to be with a band or anything. Can't you just sit down at a piano and play me a song?"

Stella let out a little laugh. "Yeah, I guess I could," she said. "If we ever see a piano laying around."

"We have plenty of them around here."

She gave him a shy smile that made him stand up a little straighter. He felt a sort of primal pride. His fists clinched at the sight of her smile, like he would do anything to protect her—to keep her smiling like that.

"I don't sing or anything," she warned. "But I'd love to play you a song sometime, if you ever want to just hear a piece on the piano."

"What kind of song would you play?" he asked, scanning her face and trying not to get too wound-up.

She shrugged. "Probably something classical."

Caleb envisioned Stella sitting at a grand piano, staring at the keys and playing a classical piece. He wondered if she sat upright or if she moved and swayed with the music.

He was around people all the time. He spoke to people one-on-one and in large groups. His life consisted of interacting with others in various capacities. Yet he never, ever felt this tripped-up, this tongue-tied, this affected.

His heart was constantly pounding when he was around her. He had spent his life in strictly platonic relationships, and now that he had eyes for a woman, he found it difficult to be cool.

"I wonder how you..." Caleb hesitated. He was so distracted that he almost came out and told her he wondered *how she sat when she was at the piano.* "I was wondering if you were going to come back to this next week," he corrected.

It was the first and only thing he had said that could be perceived as flirtatious, but he couldn't help himself. He had to show some interest in seeing her again. It was almost time to leave. Everyone was throwing away pizza boxes and wrapping up. Before

Stella could answer his question about coming back next week, a lady came up to talk to Caleb. Once she opened the flood gate, several others followed, coming up to him one-after-another for ten minutes or so.

Stella almost left.

A few different times, she made eye contact with him, and he could tell she was poised to leave, but Caleb widened his eyes just enough that she got the picture and stuck around. He turned to her right after he said goodbye what seemed to be the last person in line to talk to him.

"Thank you," he said, referring to her waiting.

"I think I'll come back next week," she said answering his question even though it had been a long time since he asked it. Stella looked around nervously. "Today was the first time I've come to church in a while," she added.

"Really?" he asked the question even though he already knew as much.

"Yeah. I haven't... I wanted to tell you... I was thinking about what you were saying today, and... I got saved and baptized and everything years ago, but I haven't ever really led a... Christ-centered life. Anyway, I don't know. I was thinking about it and I felt like I wanted to draw nearer to... God... you know, make some changes to try to put God first and everything." She shook her head with a self-deprecating smile. "I don't know what I'm saying. I guess I just wanted to say thank you. Thank you for everything you said today, and for... doing what you're doing. You're making a difference in people's lives with what you're saying up there. I felt the benefits of that today."

Caleb's heart was pounding so violently in his chest that he could hear his own heartbeat He wanted to take a hold of her. He wanted to hold her in his arms. It took every ounce of his self-restraint to keep from reaching out and touching her.

"Thank you for saying that," he said. "It means a lot. It really does. I love hearing that."

"So, yeah, I'll come back next week. I'm going to try to come more. I hope I can get in the habit of it."

"You can," he said with a shrug. "You just decide to come and you come."

"Okay, well I guess I'll see you next week," she said.

He smiled. "I really hope so."

"Hey, I know you're just moving back to town, so if you ever n-need anything... I mean, I know y-you have family here and everything, but you're welcome to... call me... if you ever need anything or even if you want to meet some people to hang out with or whatever. I have a lot of friends."

Caleb's chest felt like it might explode. She was nervous, and the sight of it made him feel overjoyed and overprotective and a whole host of other emotions he never experienced with women.

"I don't know if I have your phone number written down," he said, trying to seem way more casual than he felt. "You could maybe email me with your number. My email is Caleb Gray at Grace Church dot org. It's really easy."

"Okay, I'll email you," she said, nodding and starting to walk away.

"Send it to me when you get to the car so you don't forget," he said.

Stella went over and hugged Danny and Silvia before making her way to the door. Caleb watched her walk away, and she turned and waved at him just before stepping outside.

Chapter 8

Stella

The memory of the awkward statement rang in my head long after I said it.

"Hey, I know you're just moving back to town, so if you ever n-need anything..." It was perhaps the dorkiest monologue in history. I had said he should call me *if he needed anything,* and I just kept thinking about how connected Caleb was and how I was probably the last person he would call if he ever needed anything. Caleb had grown up in Lexington. His father was the pastor at a huge, flourishing church, and he was pretty much the most popular guy there.

Even the next day, I blushed when I thought of that conversation. The worst part was that I had done what he told me and I emailed him from the parking lot after I walked outside. Maybe I wouldn't be overanalyzing things had I heard back from that email, but I hadn't. I knew we had a good conversation where we laughed and talked to each other, but I just kept remembering how silly I must have sounded when I told him he should just call since he just moved back to town. He probably had women giving him their phone numbers left and right.

It was Sunday evening when I emailed him, and I had checked my email every waking hour since. Nothing. Nothing from Caleb at least. I had plenty of junk mail from Wayfair, Old Navy, and Bed Bath and Beyond, but nothing from Caleb.

It was five o'clock the following afternoon when my phone rang. It was a local area code, but the number wasn't saved to my contacts.

Caleb wasn't my first thought.

I thought he was going to email me.

I answered my phone, assuming it was a parent of one of my students.

"Hello?"

"Hey, is this Stella?"

His voice was deep and familiar. He was a public speaker, so it was clear and obvious. My whole body felt alive with a fluttering sensation.

"Yes," I said, biting my lip afterward and trying to control a smile.

"Hey, Stella, this is Caleb. Gray. From the church. Grace Church."

"I had it with Caleb," I said.

He laughed. I heard a low chuckle on the phone, and it made me smile.

"You said to call if I ever needed anything," Caleb said.

"Y-yes I did," I answered. "Do you need something?"

"I actually, uh, need, could use your help at the church. I didn't know if you knew we were decorating for Christmas."

"No, I didn't."

"Well, I mean, we do that every year. It's nothing new. But I didn't know if you saw in the bulletin that we were looking for volunteers. It's happening this week—today through Thursday from four to six. It's a smaller group than the ones who do the boxes."

"It already started, though, right?" I glanced at the clock even though I knew it was 5pm.

"It already started today, but it's happening other days, too. I just didn't know if you knew about it."

"No, I didn't. I think I saw something about it in the bulletin, but I—did you need my help with it, or were you just telling me it was an option?"

"Both," he said. "You said I should call if I ever needed anything, and so, yes, we could use your help, but I was also just saying it was an option. I know you mentioned wanting to get more involved at the church."

"Did you say it was just a few people?" I asked.

"Not a ton. Miss Becky is heading it up."

"Do you go to it?" I asked.

"No. I wasn't planning on it. I'm not there tonight, but if you were thinking about doing it, then I'd probably meet you up there—just to show you where to go and everything."

"What time did you say it was?" I asked.

"Four to six."

"Can I just pick a day and show up?"

"You can sign-up on line, but you don't need to. You can do as much or as little as you want. You don't have to do it at all. I was just, you know... letting you know it was happening."

"I'll go if you go," I said.

"Sure," he said with a smile in his voice. "That's great. That's why I called. What day?"

"Tomorrow?" I asked.

"Yes. Tuesday at four," he said as if wanting me to confirm.

"Yeah," I said, even though I had a piano lesson at four o'clock that I would have to reschedule. "Should I just show up at the church?" I asked. "Will it be obvious where I need to go?"

"Yes. I'll meet you there at four," he said. "In the main auditorium."

"Okay, thanks," I said. "Thanks for calling."

"Thank you," he said. "I'm glad you're coming."

"Me too. I love Christmas."

There was a brief pause, and I knew we were about hang up, but he said, "I was thinking about you today. I was wondering how Tyler did for you."

Tyler was my most challenging student.

"He was, he was okay. He was fine. It's going be fine. His mom said they were just getting the medicine dialed-in. It'll get better," I said. "I did pray for patience."

"Did that help?"

"I don't know. I think it did. It was still a long day, but the act of praying about it helped some. It kind of gave me permission to rely on something greater than myself."

"That's good," he said.

"And a few of the students told me stories from their holiday. It made me see them in a new light. A lot of them just talked about the food and the turkey or whatever, but one little boy had his family get in a huge fight where the cops came. His uncle got arrested."

"Oh man. Was it Tyler?" he asked.

"No. It was another boy. Tyler didn't mention his holiday. He doesn't say much about his home life. His mom is hard to get in touch with." I let out a whimpering sound when I realized I was venting too much. "I'm sorry," I said. "It sounds like I don't love my job, and I really do."

"It doesn't sound like that," he said. "And I'm the one who asked you about it."

"It wasn't a bad day at all," I said, trying to lighten the mood. "It was good. Thank you for asking."

"Do you want to know how my day was?" he asked after a short pause.

The question made me laugh. "Yes, actually. How was your day, preacher man?"

"I had meetings and did emails and planning in the morning, and then I finished with the roof in the afternoon. It was a good day."

"The church roof?" I asked.

"Yes. I'm not a roofer, but it wasn't a big deal. I had help."

"Are your meetings and emails and planning for church, too?"

"Yes. I'm full-time up there."

"Is that what you're going to do tomorrow?" I asked. "Will you be working all day at the church?"

"Every day except for Friday and Saturday."

"Oh, wow, I knew you worked there, but I guess I didn't realize how full-time. You don't need to meet me to decorate after you've already been there all day."

He paused for a few seconds. "I'm the one who called you, remember?" he said.

I smiled even though he couldn't see me. "Just so you don't mind," I said.

"I don't. I wouldn't have offered."

"Okay great," I said. "I guess I'll see you tomorrow at four."

"Great," he said. "I'll see you then."

We said goodbye, and I hung up the phone before heading to my parents' kitchen.

Monday was taco night at our house. We had the conversation about moving it to Tuesday to go with the popular phrase, but my dad did a lot of the cooking, and he had gotten in the habit of making them on Mondays. Mom was standing in the kitchen with him while he chopped onions and peppers.

They had music playing, and I strolled in, feeling way too happy for a Monday afternoon.

"What happened?" Mom asked me.

"What do you mean?" I asked, looking confused.

"You. What are you so happy about?"

"Me? Nothing. I mean, I got all my work done for tomorrow."

"No homework tonight?" Dad asked.

"I had some, but I finished it already. And I think I'm going to go to that decorating thing at the church tomorrow."

"What decorating thing?" Mom asked, whipping her head around to look at me.

I shrugged, acting nonchalant. "I think they're meeting to decorate the church for Christmas. It was in the bulletin."

"Really?" Mom asked. She seemed amazed and maybe a little skeptical.

"Are you surprised they're having that, or that I'm going to it?"

"That you're going," Mom said. "You went to that thing last night, too."

"I know."

"Did someone ask you to come back?"

I felt shy as a result of her question. I didn't know whether to tell the truth or not. "I told a few people that I wanted to get back into going to church, and they invited me to that decorating thing tomorrow. I saw Mr. Danny last night and a few others I recognized."

I could see the happiness in my mother's expression when I said I wanted to get back into church, and it made me feel bad about telling a half-truth.

"Caleb is a nice guy," I said, needing to shed some more light on my thoughts. "I saw him last night and I told him I hoped to start going to church more. He's the one who mentioned the decorating thing to me. I think he's looking out for me... spiritually or whatever."

"Caleb Gray?" Dad asked, chiming in.

"He's the one who told her about decorating," Mom informed him in case he hadn't heard. "He's such a nice young man. That makes me want to cry that he would look out for you."

"He might not be doing it out of the goodness of his heart," Dad said, looking up from his cutting board.

"Richard James!" Mom said, scolding him.

"What?" Dad asked, shrugging innocently. He pointed casually at me with the tip of his knife. "They're about the same age," he said. "They seem like an obvious match to me."

"Rick, stop," Mom said, shaking her head.

I, personally, thought Dad had a point, but Mom seemed to think he was joking. She looked at me, gaging my reaction.

I shrugged.

"He's a preacher," Mom said, making sure I knew. She wasn't trying to imply that I wasn't good enough for a preacher—it was more like she didn't think I would be attracted to one.

"I didn't say I wanted to go out with him," I said. "I really did start thinking about God more. I'm not saying I'm going to start going to church every time the doors open—it just happened to work out this week that there were Christmas activities to do. I'm glad he invited me. It gets my mind off work."

"I guess you two can think what you want to think, but he doesn't just take the time to show personal interest. Eight thousand people go to that church. He probably gets a hundred emails a day. He can't just take spiritual interest in all of us."

"Ricky, don't put that in her head. I don't know where you're getting that from. And I don't care if twenty-thousand people go there. He's not too busy for our baby girl. Stella wouldn't want to go out with him anyway."

"Why not?" I asked.

"Would you?" Mom asked, wearing a look of surprise.

"I wouldn't *not* go out with him," I said. "But it's not about that."

"Well, I for one am happy to see you going to church more. I don't think anyone has ulterior motives."

"I'm not saying his motives are bad," Dad said, defending himself. "I'm just saying... he's a busy man. If he makes time, he makes time. It is what it is."

"I don't know what that means," Mom said, shaking her head at my father. "But I think it's great if you'd become friends or whatever else with Caleb. As far as I'm concerned, Caleb Gray gets the go-ahead to be in your life in any capacity."

"Me too." Dad's agreement was so serious and whole hearted that it was almost comical.

"No marriage proposals quite yet," I said. "Right now, I'm just going to the church to hang some wreaths and garland. I'm not even positive that he'll be there."

Technically, it wasn't a complete lie. I wasn't *positive* he would be there since you could never be entirely positive of any future event. Still, I had no idea why I felt the need to lie. Maybe it was because they seemed excited and I didn't want them to get their hopes up.

Chapter 9

I saved Caleb's number so I knew it was him calling when my phone rang the following afternoon.

I experienced a warm rushing sensation through my body, and I took a few seconds to calm my breathing before I answered. I stared at the incoming call screen. It was quarter-till-four. I took a deep breath and answered on the third ring.

"Hello?" I said.

"Where are you?" Caleb asked.

"My parents' house. My house. Why?"

My first thought was that he had to call it off and he was trying to catch me before I left.

"I thought you'd be on your way by now. Are you still coming?"

"Yes."

"Are you on your way?"

He sounded eager to see me.

"Yes," I said, unable to contain my smile.

"It starts at four," he said. "I thought you'd be on your way by now."

"I know. I am. I'm leaving now. I'll be there at four on the dot."

I parked the car at four o'clock exactly, and only took a few seconds to glance at my reflection in the visor mirror before getting out of the car. Caleb was standing at the door when I walked up. He held it open for me, and I walked inside feeling happy and content, like there was no other way I'd want to spend a Tuesday afternoon.

We stayed stuck to each other like glue from that very first moment when he opened the door for me.

He never left my side.

We joined two other people who were decorating the main tree in the lobby. It was twenty feet tall, and Caleb and I worked on one side of it the while they worked on the other. We talked to them some, but mostly our attention was focused on one another.

I already had some sort of connection with Caleb before I went there on Tuesday, but after all of our candid conversation that night, I would definitely consider him a friend. He was an all-around amazing person. He was funny, considerate, strong, understanding, and he was oh, so handsome.

I wasn't sure if it was his connection with God or just something that came natural to him, but Caleb was a solid rock of a man—unwavering, upright. I asked him questions about God, and he answered in a down-to-earth way that made me believe the best life could only be found in serving Him.

I decided to join them at the church on Wednesday and Thursday nights as well.

I had to adjust my schedule, and I was relatively sure Caleb did as well, but neither of us mentioned that. We simply agreed that we would like to continue going to the decorating party every afternoon that week. We didn't talk on the phone, and we didn't ever mention getting together outside of church, but during those two hours, we focused our attention on each other. Christmas music was playing, and we sang and acted silly in the midst of conversations.

We had moments of seriousness and moments of playfulness, and by Thursday, I was both elated and full of dread. I was elated at the fact that I had gotten to know such a cool guy, and full of dread that our regular meetings were over.

I would always see him again on Sunday. We had already mentioned doing the Sunday evening box-stuffing party again, so I knew I had that to look forward to. It was ridiculous, but I had seen him so frequently recently that waiting until Sunday now seemed like a long time.

The start of our time apart would be here all too soon. I glanced at my watch and took in the time. It was ten minutes until six on Thursday, which meant it was almost time to leave. If the previous evenings were any indication as to how things would go tonight, we would wrap it up at six o'clock sharp. Becky was extremely organized and we had already begun tidying up in preparation to leave.

I felt like I had to establish the next time I would see him. I knew he wasn't speaking again Sunday morning. "I guess I'll see you Sunday night if I don't run into you at the morning service."

"I thought we were just talking about food, though," he said glancing at me curiously.

"We w-were," I said. Caleb and I had, indeed, been talking about food earlier. He had been in London long enough that he didn't know of half the restaurants I mentioned in Lexington.

"I thought you were tempting me for something to eat tonight," he said.

My face fell as I tried to make out what he was saying. *Food. Was he talking about us eating together tonight?* My look of confusion made Caleb laugh. The flash of white teeth along with the deep sound of his chuckle had my knees weak.

"You were talking about so many great restaurants that I just assumed we would need to eat something after this. It is dinner time. I thought that was why you were mentioning it."

"It was you who brought up food earlier," I said.

"Was it? Hmm. Okay. Well, still, I thought we'd go eat after this."

"You did?" I asked. I glanced around. People were walking along with us in the hall, but they were all in groups engaged in their own conversations. "Tonight?"

"Yes. Right after this. Since it's dinner time."

"Just us or what?"

"Is that a problem?" he asked.

"No, no. I wasn't... I didn't... sure we can," I said.

I had work to finish tonight, but that wasn't going to stop me from having dinner with Caleb. My heart raced with anticipation at the thought of continuing our evening. There was no way I would say no.

"Where do you want to go?" I asked.

"I was thinking Tony's or Bluegrass Diner."

"Let's do the diner," I said. "I could go for a cup of coffee."

"Yeah, me too," Caleb said, nodding.

We walked to the parking lot together, but we decided to drive separately since the diner was closer to his house than mine. Caleb lived in the guest house of a rich couple who had a mansion near downtown. He told me where he lived, and I could picture it perfectly because I had been to that couple's house before.

People at the church saw us walk to the parking lot together and leave at the same time. They noticed our proximity for sure. I could see for the past three afternoons that they noticed. We showed up together and stayed together the whole time we decorated. I wanted to mention the fact that we had been stared at curiously, but that would seem like I was making more out of it than it was.

I was thinking about it as we sat in our places across from each other in the booth. It was chilly out but warm inside, and I took off my jacket and set it next to me on the bench seat. Caleb was looking at me, smiling. There was an edge of barely contained mischief in that smile, and it made me instinctually smile and shake my head.

"What?"

"I don't know," I said. "I didn't expect us to get food tonight. This is a surprise."

"Well, you can't talk about the best chicken and dumplings you've ever had and expect me to go home and eat a bowl of cereal for dinner."

"Is that what you would have eaten for dinner if we didn't come here?" I asked.

He shrugged. "I'll eat bowls of cereal randomly, but normally not for a whole meal. Usually, if I do breakfast for dinner, it's fried eggs."

"Will you be having fried eggs this evening?" Our waitress showed up just in time to hear Caleb mention them. She put menus in front of us before setting down two napkins and some silverware.

"No, ma'am not tonight," Caleb said. "Fried eggs are what I make for myself when I'm not in the mood to cook. That's what I fall back on."

"Oh. We can't have you eatin' your fall back meal," she said, smiling.

"Exactly," Caleb said. "I hear I should try the chicken and dumplings, anyway."

"That's a popular one," she said. "Would you like me to go ahead and take your orders, or should I get your drinks and give you a minute to decide?"

"We'll take two cups of coffee and a minute to decide," Caleb said.

"Sure thing, she said with a nod. "I'm Lucy. I'll be taking care of you tonight."

She seemed nervous as she glanced toward the kitchen. I looked that way to find that all of the guys in the kitchen were looking our way.

"And Reggie told me to tell you your dinner is on the house tonight. We saw you come in. Several of us go to your church. Including me. When I can. I work most Sundays so I watch it on online. Anyway, Reggie said you can consider this dinner a welcome home gift."

"You guys don't have to do that," Caleb said.

"We want to," she said, bowing nervously. "Reggie already insisted, and he's the manager."

"Well, thank you. I really appreciate that," Caleb said.

Lucy smiled as she turned to leave. "I'll be right back with your coffee."

My eyes widened when Caleb and I made eye contact. "Free dinners and whatnot," I said, looking impressed.

"This is new to me, too," he said.

"Did you not have fans in London?"

"No, I didn't," he said. "I mean, I was student pastor at a church and my congregation liked me and everything, but no. My dad's church is about six times the size of the one I was working at in London. I rarely got free food over there."

"But you did get it sometimes?" I asked, since he said rarely instead of never.

He smiled. "Yeah, I guess I did get it sometimes."

"Maybe that's a thing," I said. "Maybe people like to feed pastors. Cops get discounts and free meals too. Maybe you guys fit into a similar category. Public servant."

Caleb grinned at that. He leaned back in the booth, regarding me. "Or it could just be a welcome home meal like she said."

I shrugged, leaning back in my seat to match his naturalness. "Maybe," I said. "Still, you can't deny that the first time we met, I gave you about thirty pounds of ham and casserole."

Caleb laughed at that. "I can't deny that," he said.

Lucy walked up to our table carrying two mugs and a carafe of coffee. She poured us each a cup and began talking to us about our order. She recommended the meatloaf, so we ordered that and the chicken and dumplings.

She heard about our plans to share the meals and said that Reggie would split the plates for us. I had shared a ton of meals in restaurants, and I had never had them offer to split it up on the plate for us. She catered to Caleb like he was a celebrity. I had seen it happen to my uncle, but it was unexpected with Caleb.

In spite of the special treatment, we enjoyed a fun, quiet, down-to-earth dinner. I had never been shy when it came to eating in front of guys, and I went ahead and ate to my heart's content. I almost cleaned my plate. Caleb did clean his, and he made a solemn vow, as he was doing it, to come back to this establishment on a regular basis. We talked about other meals we had in different cities, and an hour passed in what seemed like seconds.

Lucy asked if we saved room for dessert and insisted that if we had any room at all, we needed to try the peanut butter pie. She said if we didn't have room then she would pack us a slice to take home. Caleb told her we would love to try it and that we would eat it there at the restaurant.

I was stuffed and couldn't imagine taking another bite of food, but I was glad Caleb had agreed to eat dessert because it meant he wasn't in a hurry.

We were waiting for the pie when Caleb mentioned the jukebox. I had heard a few songs playing while we ate, and I was even aware they had a jukebox, but it had completely slipped my mind.

I loved jukeboxes. I knew I had to choose some songs the instant he mentioned it. I dug in my purse for a couple of dollar bills and jogged over to it, feeling excited about choosing a song.

It was a digital jukebox with a touchscreen, but there were lots of oldies and classic songs to choose from. I loved oldies and knew all of the songs flashing on the screen as I scrolled through the options.

I had three plays, and I chose "My Girl," without hesitation as selection number one.

I smiled when I saw a Dusty Springfield song called *Son of a Preacher Man*. I had heard the song so many times that the first verse popped into my head without even having to think about it. It was an iconic first line.

Billy Ray was a preacher's son,
and when his daddy would visit he'd come along.

It did not escape me that the name of the boy in the song, Billy Ray, was easily interchangeable with Caleb Gray. I sang the first verse with Caleb's name naturally inserted in Billy Ray's place, and I smiled giddily at how well it fit and how relevant the whole song was to me.

The lyrics also talked about him sweet talking a girl and kissing her.

That was me, of course.

I blushed.

It was for this reason that I did not play the song. It would be so obvious that I had feelings for him if I had. I chose to ignore the glorious lyrical coincidence and instead went for the next two songs that I liked.

I chose *Sir Duke* by Stevie Wonder and *Oh! Darling* by the Beatles.

Chapter 10

Caleb

It was a real struggle for Caleb to remain cool with Stella. He found that it was almost impossible to behave with her like he did with everyone else.

There was no shortage of women in his life, and he never had a problem with maintaining friendship-level relationships with them. But he was having real trouble with Stella.

He wanted her in his life, and he was convinced that she was meant for him, so it was like pushing against the current for him to reign it in and take things slowly.

If it were up to him, he'd just marry her now and start a life—just go to the same house, beginning tonight. Caleb took a deep, measured breath at the thought. He stared at her profile while she was across the room, pushing buttons on the jukebox.

The song *My Girl* came over the speakers, and Caleb smiled at her choice. The server brought two slices of pie to their table and poured more coffee into their mugs. He thanked her, and by the time she headed away, Stella was on her way back to the table.

Caleb smiled at her as she approached. She was grinning, and her eyes widened with delight when she noticed that the pie was sitting on the table.

"She brought apple and peanut butter," Caleb said. "I was going to let you choose."

Stella stared at the plates with an excitement that made Caleb smile.

"Yum. I thought we were just getting peanut butter," Stella said.

"She said Reggie's favorite is apple and he sent it over."

"I don't know which one looks better," she said. "Which one do you want? I could split them up again. Really, I just want a bite of each of them."

He nudged his chin at her, grinning. "Why don't you just take what you want off of both of them and leave me the rest."

Stella smiled and began cutting into the pie without hesitation. "Sir Duke," he said, noticing the iconic opening horn line of the second song. He liked Stevie Wonder and knew the song within the first few notes. "Nice choice."

Stella looked up from her pie-cutting and gave him an excited smile. "I love jukeboxes," she said. "I'm sad that we didn't find it until after our meal. I knew it was here, and I forgot. I would have played about twenty songs by now."

She handed Caleb a plate with the lion's share of pie, and he took it without mentioning the discrepancy in portions.

"What's so good about a jukebox?" He looked at her in such a way that she knew his question was lighthearted and meant to get to know her better.

She danced in her seat, the small movements of her shoulders going to the beat of the song. "Because," she said. "How often do you get to pick the music everyone listens to at a restaurant? Never. I don't know why there aren't more jukeboxes in the world. They're the most fun ever."

She stared at him and her shoulder movements intensified a little as if to drive home her point.

Caleb laughed. "How many did you choose?"

"Just one more after this one," she said. "It was three for a dollar. I almost put two dollars in, but I figured we were almost done."

Caleb did not want to part ways with her, he wanted to stare into her bright green eyes for the rest of the night and then for every night after that. As it stood, the next time he would see her would be Sunday, and that was completely unacceptable.

"Beatles?" he asked a minute later when the third song came on.

She shrugged. "I figured you might be homesick for the great-British-land," she said.

She spoke in a hilariously thick British accent. She was fully committed to it, and Caleb could not hold in a laugh. Also, it struck him as funny that she called it great-British-land.

"Are you having a laugh at me?" Stella asked, straight-faced, but still speaking in that accent.

"No, never," Caleb said innocently as he took a bite of pie.

"Do you miss it?" she asked in her real voice. She was precious and curious. Caleb stared at her knowing he would be with her for the rest of his life.

"No," he said.

"No? Not at all?"

"No," he said. "I had some people I was close to—people I love and I'll miss, but I'm really only a short flight from there. I promised I'd go back to visit. This is my home. If I was going to be homesick for any place, it'd be here."

"Good," she said. "Home is where the heart is, anyway."

Caleb didn't know what she meant by it. Stella shrugged and took a bite of her pie like she wasn't really sure what she meant by it either.

Reggie came by to tell Caleb how happy he was that he came to eat at the diner. He told Caleb that he should come back with his father sometime, and Caleb agreed that he would. He thanked Reggie for the meal and the special treatment, and he left a twenty-dollar tip for Lucy.

Caleb walked outside with Stella, hating that they were about to part ways. They were in a downtown building and their vehicles were parked in a nearby public parking lot. They headed that direction, but they were not in a hurry. They walked so slowly it could barely be categorized as walking.

"I think there's more decorating that needs to happen," he said, feeling desperate to see her again.

"Really?" she asked. "At the church? Like with Becky?"

"No."

"What then? Where?"

"Nothing. There's actually nothing that needs to be decorated. I completely made that up just now."

"Well, if you guys figure out that you need any more help decorating... I really had fun doing that."

Caleb wanted to have her come decorate his office or his apartment. *Was that inappropriate?* He didn't even know anymore when it came to Stella. Lines felt blurred. He didn't know how much he could say to her when nothing shy of *will you marry me* seemed sufficient.

"When I was a kid, I spent a lot of time in this building," he said, stopping in front of an ornate set of doors. "There was a set of escalators in it, and I rode up and down it what must have been five hundred times as a kid. Maybe more. I could probably actually figure out the exact number of times if you gave me a minute to do some math in my head."

"How in the world would you do that?" she asked.

"My dad let me ride up and down them no more than ten times a day when I came up here with him. I came during the summer for three or four years. He had an office for counseling on the second floor." He paused and smiled at her. "I'm not going to sit here and think about it and do the math, but I rode that escalator a lot of times, let's put it that way. If it was open, I'd go ride it again right now for old time's sake."

Before they could walk off, Stella reached out and pulled the door, and her eyebrows rose when it opened.

"It's dark in there," he said. "They're closed."

"The businesses are, but the building's not."

She lifted her eyebrows as she went inside. Caleb followed her. He was a rule-follower from way back, and the building was clearly closed. The inside was like a mall, and he could see the darkness and the closed storefronts from the door.

"Which way is the escalator?" she asked, walking inside with no trepidation whatsoever.

"That way, but..." Caleb pointed toward his left, and Stella instantly grinned and headed down the hall in that direction. She was fearless.

They passed a man on their way—a janitor who was mopping in front of a closed store. Stella smiled, waved at him, and walked by as if she knew right where she was going. He didn't wave back, but he also didn't stop them.

The escalators were there in the same secluded spot just like Caleb remembered. It was nice seeing them and everything, but they were shut off for the evening.

"We can use them as stairs," Stella said, going to the base of them. She tilted her head. "I wonder if this one goes up or down."

"Up," Caleb said.

"How do you know?"

"I remember. Like I said, I rode them hundreds of times. I used to go up the down one, and that's the one over there. You have to go twice as fast when you do that."

He scanned the length of it. "Back then, it felt like Mount Everest."

Stella smiled as she, too, peered up the stairs. It was an older, small set—vintage. "I wish you could ride up and down one time," she said. "For old time's sake." She leaned over and glanced down the hall in the direction from which they had come. "Maybe that man could turn it on for us," she said even though they had turned a corner and he was no longer in sight.

"No, it's okay," Caleb said.

"It might just be the touch of a button," Stella said. She leaned over and looked at the escalator itself as if searching for a switch. She was tenacious, and it both delighted and frightened Caleb. It mostly delighted him.

Before he knew it, Stella had talked him into letting her take a shot at sweet-talking the janitor.

Carl was his name.

He wasn't having any part of being sweet-talked at first. In fact, he seemed annoyed. He asked what they were doing there, and Caleb thought for sure they were about to get kicked out.

But Stella was good. She was charming. She told the guy the whole true story about Caleb going there as a kid and said he had just moved back to town. She only said a few simple things to the guy. She didn't even try to name drop Caleb's dad or her uncle.

And somehow, the guy went from being agitated to being eager to please. He led them back to the escalator, smiling and saying things about his own childhood memories.

He had to use a key to turn it on, but it only took him a few seconds.

"Y'all be good. No getting shoe laces stuck in there."

"Yes sir," Stella assured him. "We'll only be five or ten minutes, and we'll go out the way we came in."

He was smiling and looking happy with himself for doing a good deed as he went back to his chores.

"How did you do that?" Caleb asked once the guy had walked away.

"I didn't, Carl did," she said. "Turns out, you do have to have a key."

He smiled. "How did you get Carl to do it?" he asked.

"I just asked," she said with a shrug. "He was nice."

"Yes, he was," Caleb agreed.

His attention shifted to the escalators. The two of them stood at the bottom of the set of stairs that were now moving upward.

"After you, my lady," Caleb said, gesturing for Stella to go ahead.

She stepped onto the bottom step and felt it move under her feet. Quickly, she brought the other foot up so they were both resting on the same step. Caleb climbed onto the step directly below her, and she turned to the side so she could talk to him.

"This is a cool escalator," she said, looking around.

"It's smaller than I remember, but it's the same, too. It even smells the same."

"How long has it been since you've come here?"

"Like fifteen or twenty years."

"You're kidding," she said.

"No, I was little."

It was a short ride to the top, and before they knew it, Stella was stepping onto the second floor. It was a speckled tile floor that was probably installed in the fifties. Stella liked the looks of the place and the smell of it. She waited for him at the top, and he stepped off of the escalator seconds later.

"My dad's office was right there," he said, pointing at a storefront.

Stella's eyes drifted upward and she read the sign. It was a massage therapy place now.

"They went from regular therapy to massage therapy," she said.

"Looks like it," Caleb agreed.

He followed Stella as she walked around the balcony to the place where the escalator went down. "Are you ready to go down?" Caleb asked when she hesitated near the top.

"I figured we'd go ahead and ride ten times," she said. "Since it's tradition."

"It is tradition," Caleb agreed, feeling thankful for any excuse to stay with her. They rode up and down the escalator nine more times, going slow and talking as they went.

Chapter 11

Stella

We rode up and down the escalator ten times. Caleb always let me get on in front of him, but I reversed our roles on the very last time riding down. I knew it was the last leg of our escalator adventure, and I wanted to do something unexpected.

I stood back gesturing for Caleb to get on ahead of me.

Neither of us had been giving any thought or consideration to the mechanics of walking and riding the escalators. We had been focused on talking and telling stories. Caleb hadn't been expecting me to tell him to go first, so he didn't have time to think about it. He just stepped onto the escalator ahead of me.

He turned, expecting me to get on with him, but I didn't. I just watched him ride downward. He was about three feet away from me when his expression changed to one of question.

"Are you staying up there?" he asked as he slowly, smoothly drifted away from me.

"Would you miss me if I did?" I asked.

It was officially flirty, but he would be driving away in minutes and I had to pull out all the stops.

"Yes, I would," he said. "I can't just leave you up there. If you won't come down, I'll have to go up after you."

I grinned at the thought. "That's what I wanted you to do," I said. "You said you liked to go up the down escalator. I want you to put your money where your mouth is."

"You want me to climb back up this set?" he asked in surprise.

I nodded at him as he grew farther and farther away.

"You know it'll take me about three-and-a-half seconds," he said confidently.

That sounded like the men in my family, and it made me laugh. "Okay, show me, big shot."

Caleb stood on the first floor looking up at me. I could see his whole body—head to toe. There was nothing between us besides a moving set of stairs. He shook his head at me before taking off.

Caleb was absolutely accurate when he estimated how many seconds it took him to make it back to me. One second, I was staring down at him, and the next, he was flying up the stairs.

He came to a smooth but abrupt stop as soon as his feet hit the floor at the top. His momentum was so great and I was so close to the edge that he almost ran into me. I could have stepped back, but I didn't. I held my ground, letting him crowd my space. I wanted more than anything for him to just take a hold of me and draw me into his arms. I wanted him to hold me tightly. His chest rose and fell as he took a deep breath, looking down at me.

"That was seriously only three seconds," I said, staring up at him.

He smiled. "I told you."

"I thought you were over-exaggerating."

"Nope."

"You're barely even winded from that," I said, taking in the fact that his breathing wasn't even labored.

"Oh, I'm in bad shape," he said.

"What? You're not even breathing heavy."

"Yeah, but I'm not doing so well. I'm burning up."

"Burning up?"

He nodded. "I think it's fever."

"Fever?" My expression was confused, and he shrugged.

"Maybe so. Yeah, I think I have a fever. You should check."

"My hands are cold," I said, feeling my own forehead with the back of my fingers.

"Just check," he said.

I had gotten to know him enough in the last week to recognize when he was being playful even if he had a serous expression.

I wanted to touch him, but it was difficult for me to reach out and do it. "You don't have a fever," I said, shaking my head a little and squinting at him suspiciously. In spite of my trepidation, I reached up and placed my hand on his forehead. I used the palm-side of my fingers instead of the outside like I had done on my own forehead. My touch was ever so tentative. Caleb leaned down a little, pressing his forehead against my hand so I could get a more secure reading. When he did, his whole face came closer to mine.

My body was alive with anticipation.

He was only a foot or two away.

"You do feel a little warm," I said, when his temperature registered on my fingertips. I made a curious expression and checked my own head again. "No, actually. You feel the same as me," I corrected.

"Are you sure?" he asked.

"Yeah. I'm just as warm as you are."

I kept my hand on my own forehead, nodding and feeling certain about my temperature-comparing skills.

"Okay, if you think so," he said in a doubtful tone. He wanted me to touch him again, but we were both being discreet about it, and I felt shy.

"Let me check one more time," I said, unable to stand it. I reached up and placed my fingertips on his forehead again. He stared at me as I did it. I gazed at my own hand. Caleb's dark eyes we're locked on me so intently that it was difficult for me to look directly into them.

I made a thoughtful expression like I was really trying to tell whether or not he was warm. We both knew this whole thing was a charade. Maybe this sort of innocence wouldn't appeal to some people, but honestly, it caused warm waves of desire to flow through my body. I absolutely loved the way he moved so slowly—got to know me. I brought my hand downward, cupping his cheek in my palm, and still making a face like I was trying to take his temperature from a second location like my mom did to me.

Really, I wasn't thinking about how warm he was at all. I was too busy being distracted by the electricity that flowed through me as a result of my hand touching his face. His face and jaw felt big in my hand, and my heart pounded as I hesitated for a few seconds, touching him, faking it. Finally, I pulled my hand away.

"No," I said. "I think you feel good. Normal."

He smirked. "Hmm, that's funny because I don't feel normal. I might not have a fever, but I'm definitely not normal right now."

For several seconds, we stared at each other. I knew what both of us wanted. Let me take that back. I knew what I wanted, and I hoped it was what he wanted too. I thought it was. I was relatively sure we were barely refraining from kissing each other.

"We should go," I said. "Carl's going to wonder what happened." I hated myself for breaking the silence, but I was nervous about letting it happen.

"I know," Caleb said. "You ready?"

I nodded, and then I watched as Caleb turned and stepped onto the escalator.

"Are you coming with me this time?" he asked.

But I was already stepping onto it by the time he spoke.

We thanked Carl on our way out.

Caleb let me walk ahead of him and held doors for me like a real gentleman.

We did not hold hands or make any sort of contact as we walked, but our posture and vibe made it seem like we were on the verge of it the whole time. The air between us was so charged that I knew we had mutual feelings.

We were flirtier tonight than we had ever been. It wasn't the cheesy type of flirtatiousness where I giggled and batted my eyes, either. It was like we were allowing ourselves to look at each other differently. Our gazes were less guarded. Our intentions were made clearer.

On our way back to our vehicles, we speculated about the possibility of Carl catching Caleb going up the down elevator, and Caleb said the fear of that was what helped him make it to the top so quickly. We laughed about how fast he had done it and said he floated to the top without his feet touching the stairs. It had long since been dark out, and I needed to get home to prepare for school the following day. Caleb knew that was the case. He walked me to my car.

"I guess I'll see you Sunday," he said as we came to stand next to the driver's door. "Thanks for helping out at the church and for letting me take you to dinner. Or, I guess Reggie took both of us to dinner. But thanks for coming."

"Thank you for asking me," I said. "I had fun."

I unlocked my car, and I reached for the handle. My heart raced as I opened the door. I knew it was about to happen. I knew I was going to kiss him. It was going to be quick, but I had plans to pop up and put my lips on his cheek before getting into my car. I had to do it. I had to let him know what I was feeling. That way the ball would be in his court. If I didn't hear from him until Sunday when I saw him at church then I would go back to friendship barriers.

I went for it.

I didn't hesitate.

I ignored the nerves, and as I opened my car door, I swung back, stepping toward him and leaning upward. My aim was on point and I hit this side of his mouth, I mostly got his cheek, but I touched the very edge of his lip. I barely had time to notice that, though, because our contact was chaste. I pulled back. I smiled at him for a split second but quickly broke eye contact as I kept my momentum and went to sit in the driver's seat. "Bye," I said, glancing at him one last time before I closed the door.

I started my car and instantly rolled down the window when I saw that he was still standing there. He placed his hand on top of my car and he leaned down and peered inside.

"So, I'll see you Sunday, at church," I said, acting like nothing had happened even though my heart was beating like crazy.

"Yeah, but if I need anything between now and then, I'll call you, okay?"

I nodded, trying to play it cool. "Sure. You can just call if you need anything," I said.

Within seconds, I was on the road headed home. When I drove away, Caleb had been staring at my car, looking awestruck and speechless. I knew he felt a reaction to my kiss, and it made me feel giddy to see him stare at me like that afterward. He was handsome and sturdy, like a mighty oak. I could clearly picture how handsome and noble he looked as I drove away, and the thought of it made me want to squeal. I shook the steering wheel, and since it was in one fixed position, it shook me instead.

I blasted the radio on my way home, listening to pop music and singing along with as many lyrics as I knew. I took a shower and then settled in for some last-minute lesson planning.

It was nearly two hours later when I headed to the kitchen to get some juice and I overheard my mother and brother having a conversation about me. I wasn't planning on eavesdropping, but I hesitated in the hallway when I heard them mention me by name. I would have kept going and joined them if it had been a regular conversation about me, but it was Tanner who was speaking and it sounded a little, for lack of a better word… judge-y.

"Why's Stella going to church so much?" he asked.

"I don't know," Mom said. "She volunteered to help them decorate for Christmas, I think. Dad thinks she's interested in the pastor's son."

Tanner made a dismissive, "Pfft," sound when she said that. "Yeah right."

I could clearly hear them, and I stood still, afraid to move in either direction.

"Why do you say that?" my mom asked, sounding offended and reading my mind.

"Stella would not date a preacher."

My little brother made the statement with such certainty that it made my eyebrows furrow. I felt offended at first, and then I realized that my behavior would lead him to believe that I would be a terrible fit for a preacher.

I was no stranger to nightlife. I knew what it was to live for the weekend, and my brother knew about some of the partying I'd done in the past.

Maybe I was a terrible fit for a preacher.

That had never occurred to me.

I just assumed I could change and everything would be okay. I had changed. It had only been a few days, but partying had lost its appeal to the extent that I had almost forgotten I ever had any interest in it. Sitting across from Caleb in that diner and riding escalators with him was way better than going out.

"Well, then maybe she's going to the church because she's getting closer to God," Mom said. "I think either way, it's positive."

I couldn't take it any longer. I wasn't the type to hide from confrontation. I took off walking at a brisk pace and rounded the corner like I hadn't been standing still in the hallway.

"You were asking about me going to church?" I asked, looking straight at my little brother as I came into the room.

He was across the way, sitting on a barstool near the end of the kitchen counter. Mom was standing on the adjacent side of the counter, talking to him while he ate a plate of food. It was a normal position for them. Mom used the times when Tanner was refueling to talk to him for a few minutes.

"Yeah, I was asking why you were always up at the church lately."

"Why does it matter?" I asked.

"Because Phil Cason's big brother was asking about you. He said you were supposed to hang out with Lexi and them tonight but you canceled."

"I did cancel," I said.

"Mom said it was because you went up to the church," Tanner noted.

"I did."

"That's like ten days in a row."

"No, it's not," I said. "And I can go to church every day of my life and even date a preacher if I want," I said defiantly, like a true big sister.

"So, you are dating that guy?" Tanner asked.

"No. But I can if I want. And I can start going to church all the time, too. It's fun. I decorated a gigantic Christmas tree, and I liked it."

"Was prince charming helping you decorate?" Tanner asked.

I glanced at my mom who was no help at all— she just shrugged and stared at me like she was waiting for me to answer.

"That's none of your business," I said.

"He was," Tanner said. He took a bite of food with a deadpan expression. "She's in love with a preacher," he said.

"No," I said. "I like him a little or whatever, but it's more than that. It's God too. It's taking away from what I feel about God to say I'm just up there checking out a guy."

I had used a serious, sincere tone when I said it, and Tanner looked at me with a surprised expression. "Oh, okay, so you're getting all churched-up right now." Tanner was making fun of me a little, but I didn't care.

"Yep, I'm getting all churched-up," I said defiantly.

"Amen to that," Mom said.

Chapter 12

I was confident in front of my brother, but that night when I was in bed, my thoughts got the better of me.

What if Tanner's reaction to me dating a preacher meant that I was not good enough? What if other people reacted that way? I hadn't even thought of that before. I assumed that I could just come back to God and to church like the prodigal I was and start fresh. I didn't even consider that people might think I was not good enough for Caleb. I wondered if Caleb saw me that way.

Tanner's reaction wasn't based on me not being good enough for Caleb—he just honestly thought I would never be interested in him. I remembered back to how he scoffed and what he said, and I knew it was more about thinking I would never fall for a preacher.

But lying in bed that night, with the way my mind twisted and turned things around, I came to the conclusion that everyone in Caleb's life (his church people) might not go for him dating someone like me. I cringed when I remembered kissing him without his permission at the end of the night. I thought he had been staring at me in wonder, but maybe he wasn't. Maybe he was contemplating how forward I was being.

At the end of it all, after thinking about it for at least a couple of hours, I decided there was nothing I could do to change the actions in my past. I couldn't take back the kiss and I couldn't take back the years of questionable decisions I had made before meeting Caleb. I currently had no control of the decisions I made in my past. All I had was this point forward, and all I could do was my best.

I went to sleep that night wishing I had heard from Caleb but knowing that was too much to ask after we spent the whole evening together.

The following day was Friday, and I was happy to close out another work week. I would have two more weeks of school before another much-needed break. It had honestly been the longest eight months of my life. I had finals and graduation followed by starting work and realizing how challenging it would be. This combined with the breakup with Liam had left me reeling. Not to mention, I moved twice. It was no wonder I had found God.

I thought about God when I turned the corner into the teacher's lounge and saw a couple of friends standing there. They were two of my going-out buddies. Usually, on Friday, we liked to get together and have a few drinks while we vented about our week. I no longer felt right doing that, but at the same time, I knew I would miss them. I liked their company and we always had fun. I had already told them earlier in the week that I might not be able to hang out tonight, but as I saw them standing in the lounge, I felt a tinge of regret. I had nothing else to do tonight and I knew it would feel good to hang out with them and laugh at some of the stressful moments from our week. I was instantly at war with myself about whether or not I should go with them.

"Are you meeting us tonight?" was the first thing Danielle said to me.

"I might," I said noncommittally.

I crossed to the fridge to retrieve my dish from lunch.

"I left you a yogurt in there." I wasn't looking at them, but it was Carly who said it, I recognized her voice.

Indeed, resting right on top of my Tupperware, was a small container of cherry yogurt. My favorite. I happened to be hungry, so I took it out of the refrigerator and opened it right away, feeling thankful for thoughtful friends.

I set my dish on the counter, took a plastic spoon out of the drawer, and leaned against the counter. I took a bite of yogurt as I turned to face them. There were other teachers in the lounge, but Danielle and Carly were two of my closer friends.

"Thank you for this," I said after I took a bite.

"You're welcome," Carly said.

"We're meeting at Carly's so we can ride together," Danielle said. "Your Nick and a few of his friends are meeting us."

"Nick who? Did you say *my Nick*?" I asked.

"Yeah. The photographer," Danielle said.

Me and my teacher friends had run into my photographer friend, Nick, a few weeks ago when we were out. It was right after Liam moved.

"Yeah, I follow his Instagram," Danielle said. "I ran into him at a grocery store yesterday and I went up to him. I told him we were all going out tonight and he said he'd meet us. He kind of thinks you're coming."

"He won't care if I go or don't go," I said, assuring her they'd have fun without me. I continued eating the yogurt.

"What'd you have come up?" she asked.

I didn't want to say I wasn't in the mood to have drinks. It wasn't about me trying to be good or follow rules, it was more that I didn't have an interest in going tonight. I didn't want to say it was about God, though, and I didn't have the right to say it was about Caleb. I chose to blame it on Caleb since I thought that would offend them the least.

"There is a guy," I said. "I might or might not have some plans with a guy."

It was basically a lie, but I thought it was better than flaking out for no apparent reason.

"Oooh, who is he?" Carly asked.

I thought about it, but I could not bring myself to say Caleb's name. "He's a guy from my parents' church, believe it or not."

I instantly regretted saying that and feared that they would still think I was judging them. "If I don't end up hearing from him, I'll call you guys and go meet you," I said, trying to divert their attention. "Where are you going?"

"Jude's," Danielle said, referring to a bar.

I nodded and then I rinsed and recycled my plastic. I had on loose-fitting, pleated dress pants that gathered at the waist. My phone was in my pocket, and because of all the fabric, I wasn't sure if I had felt it vibrate or not.

"What's the matter?" Danielle asked, seeing my face as I froze in my tracks and concentrated, leaning to the side in a weird pose.

"I'm trying to feel if my phone's vibrating in my pocket." I quickly threw the yogurt container and spoon into the bin and dug for my phone.

Sure enough, I was getting a call. I saw Caleb's name right when I glanced at the phone.

"That's him right there," I explained. "I'll be back in just a minute."

I was already walking away when I said that. I pressed the button to answer the phone as I headed out of the lounge.

"Hello?" I said, walking down the hall.

"Hey, Stella."

He hesitated, but I was winded and still moving, so I didn't answer right away.

"I didn't think you would be able to pick up," he said.

"I'm on break while the kids are at PE."

I found a secluded area at the end of the hall to finish my conversation. It was near the music room and I could see into the open door and knew no one was in there at the moment.

"What are you doing?" I asked.

"I, I'm at home actually. I did that job at my parents' house this morning, but my dad helped and we wrapped it up already."

"Oh, yeah, how'd that come out?" I asked. He was helping his dad build shelves in a closet.

"It looks good," Caleb said. "My mom loves it."

"Nice," I said. "Is everything okay?" I asked, wondering why he called.

"Yeah, why?"

"Because, you know, you called."

"Oh, that. Yes. I was just going to leave you a message. I didn't think you'd pick up."

"What were you going to say on the message?"

"That I, uh, I basically... I was thinking that I didn't want to wait until I need something to call you. And that you could call me if you need anything, too. I was gonna say it better than that, but basically, I was going to say that you can call me if you need anything, too. And that we don't need to need anything to call each other."

I smiled. "Oh, so you were just calling me to tell me that we can call each other?"

"Yes. Exactly. You can and should call me. You know. Sometime. Anytime." He let out a breath. "I was planning on saying it a lot better than that on the message, though." Caleb was gloriously nervous. The guy who could captivate thousands of people from the stage was nervous and rambling. I bit my lip, leaning against the wall and feeling like a love-struck teenager.

"Your timing was impeccable just now, actually," I said. "I did need you, and you came through. Perfect timing."

"What do you mean?" he asked.

"I was looking for a way out of doing something tonight. I used you for an excuse right before you called."

"Did you tell your friends you were going somewhere with me tonight?"

I hesitated, unsure as to how to answer the direct and unexpected question. "I, no. I told them that if I didn't end up going out with them that... yes. I guess I did imply that I might have plans, but I didn't mention... I didn't use specific names or anything." As I spoke my nerves got worse and worse until, eventually, my voice was shaky and I was out of breath. I trailed off and took a quick breath and then spoke again. "No, it was just that your call was just in time."

"You shouldn't lie," he said. He spoke in such a serious tone, that for a minute I thought he was simply getting onto me.

"I'm not lying," I said.

"No, I mean you shouldn't lie to your friend. If you told your friend we made plans, then we should just go ahead and make plans. Don't you think? That way you're not lying."

I stiffened out, straight as a board against the wall. I closed my eyes tight and clenched my fists.

"Stella?"

"Yes, yes, I'm here." (Trying to sound calm.) "Yeah, I didn't know what your plans were, but that would be good on my end."

"Okay, so we'll get together this evening."

"Yes," I confirmed, my heart fluttering.

"And just so we're clear," he said. "This will not be affiliated with the church in any way."

"Yep, we're clear about that," I said.

"So, we'll just be making plans. You and me. Not with the church."

I smiled from ear to ear. I was smiling so hard that I had to flex my face to wipe the smile off it.

"I know it's not with the church," I said. "And that means we have to make plans. Either you've got to pick me up, or I can meet you somewhere. Think about it, and you can text me or—"

"I'll pick you up," he said, cutting me off. "What time?"

"Uh, as early as six," I said.

"Okay, so six," he said. "Text me your address."

"What are the plans?" I asked, wondering what I should wear.

"Dinner and a movie," he said in a matter of fact tone.

"Oh, that's what we're doing? Dinner and a movie?"

"Isn't that what people do?" he asked. "Isn't that what a first date should be? Unless you want to get wild and play some miniature golf."

I laughed. "I would seriously like to play miniature golf," I said. "I have not done that in so long."

"We could do that," he offered easily.

"Thank you, but I think I might want to see a movie," I said. "I like that idea."

"Think about it and we can decide later. Don't forget to text me your address."

"I won't," I said. "I guess I'll see you at six."

"Yes. Six o'clock," he replied. "See you then."

I smiled as I hung up, and that grin stayed on my face while I headed down the hall, back toward the lounge. Danielle and Carly were standing near the door when I came around the corner.

"Oh, hey," I said.

Carly was holding my Tupperware. "You left your dish." She held it out for me and I took it from her.

"Was that your man?" Danielle asked with a smirk.

I gave her a little shrug. "He's taking me to a movie," I said.

"Ooh, a moo-vie," she said. "Why don't y'all meet us afterward? We're gonna be out late."

"I'll ask him," I said. I nodded sincerely like it was a good option, but I was pretty much positive we wouldn't go.

Chapter 13

My dad was the only one at the house later that evening when Caleb came to pick me up. I had told him I was going out, but he had long since stopped asking me for details, so he had no idea where I was headed or what time I was leaving.

He and I had been catching up in the kitchen, but he went to his bedroom a few minutes before and was in there when I saw Caleb's truck pull into the driveway. I went down the hall to let him know I wouldn't be there when he came out.

"I'm leaving!" I yelled from the other side of his closed bedroom door. I heard him yell back for me to have fun and be safe, but he didn't give any indication that he was coming out, so I turned and headed for the door. I figured I'd meet Caleb in the driveway and save him the trip inside.

I checked my reflection in the mirror on my way out. The weather was cold and I had on the outfit I wore at work that day. It was the same loose, pleated dress pants and blouse, only I added a wool coat. I had taken the time to readjust my hair and freshen my powder and lip gloss, but otherwise I looked like I had at work that day.

I could not believe my current situation. It was surreal to me that Caleb was at my house. I had somehow gone from not knowing him at all to seeing him every single day. And the strangest thing was that it seemed natural.

I must have spent more time making my way to his truck than I thought because Caleb was on the sidewalk in front of the house when I opened the door. It was only 6pm but it was dark out.

I stepped onto the porch, closing the door behind me. The porch light was on, and there were lights on the path, so I could clearly see Caleb's smiling face. His dark eyes squinted when he smiled. He was a man's man. He looked sharp and masculine—well put-together but approachable. I wanted to walk straight into his arms, but I knew we weren't at that point yet.

"Hey," I said.

"Hey."

"You ready?" I asked.

He tilted his head at me and looked past me, over my shoulder, toward my front door. "I thought I would go inside," he said. "Shouldn't I... I don't know... tell them I'll take care of you or something?"

My heart melted at his words. I felt actual warmth in my chest. He wanted to assure my family he would take care of me and it caused a warm, fluid sensation to happen.

"It's just my dad," I said. "Tanner's at basketball and my mom's helping with Piper. She's over at Justin's."

"Shouldn't I shake your dad's hand?" he asked.

Liam would have never, in a million years, asked to shake my dad's hand. He wasn't rude to my family, but he preferred to avoid interacting with them. "You can if you want," I said. I didn't mean to seem so surprised, but this wasn't a common occurrence for me. None of the guys I had dated ever wanted to meet my parents. They wanted to meet my uncle, but that was different. Caleb's self-assurance and propriety was new to me.

He gave a nod and gestured for me to turn around and go back inside, and because he was so no-nonsense about it, I did as he said. I led the way and Caleb followed me into the house.

My father was coming down the hallway when we came inside. "Hello, Mister Wilde," Caleb said.

His long stride had him crossing the living room in seconds, and he and my father converged in the space where the kitchen met the living room.

"Ricky," my dad said, shaking Caleb's hand.

My dad wasn't used to guys doing this, either, and he stood up straight, regarding Caleb with newfound respect.

"I was hoping to take your daughter to eat and see a movie."

My dad spared a tiny little glance at me like this was the strangest conversation he had ever been a part of, and my eyes widened slightly because it was strange for me, too.

"Sure," Dad said. "That sounds amazing. That sounds fun. You two should definitely do that."

"Okay, great. Thank you. Stella was saying Tanner was at basketball. Does he have a game tonight?"

"Not tonight," Dad said. "But their season just started. He's got a game tomorrow."

"Oh really? I'd like to see him play."

"You should come any time," Dad said. "We'd love to have you. Like I said, the season just started."

"Stella was telling me how good he is," Caleb said. "I'm excited to watch a game."

"Anytime," Dad said. "We go to all of them. You can just sit with us."

"All right. I appreciate it. And I'll bring your daughter home safe tonight."

"Yes. Thank you," my dad said formally, bowing a little.

Caleb turned to head toward the door, and when he did, I made eye contact with my dad. His eyes widened and we shared a brief, conspiratorial stare. I had no idea what he was trying to say, but he was definitely impressed.

"Night, Dad," I said nonchalantly.

"Night," he said. "Have fun."

Caleb opened the door for me and we walked out together. It wasn't until I was around a real gentleman that I realize how far from chivalry we as a society had come. Caleb hadn't done anything abnormal by talking to my dad, and yet it seemed so foreign. I was so utterly smitten.

129

I was relatively sure I was, indeed, not good enough for him, but I was too tenacious to let him go. I wasn't going to just give up or assume that he thought the worst of me. After all, he was the one who had mentioned going out. He was the one who came and picked me up, and he was the one who insisted on talking to my father. He seemed like he wanted to be here, as long as that was the case, I wasn't going to doubt myself or question it.

I felt all warm and fuzzy, nostalgic, like I wanted to sit next to him on a couch and cuddle up. He walked with me to the passenger side of his truck and opened the door.

This was all very date-like. To some, dinner and a movie might seem mundane, but to me it was the stuff of fairytales. We decided on seeing an action film that had just come out and we only had an hour or so to spare before it started, so we chose dinner accordingly. There was a little wood-fired pizza place near the theater that I knew would get us in and out quickly, and we ate there.

The place was packed, and we got several stares from people who I didn't recognize. I could tell they recognized Caleb, and I figured they were part of the congregation. Eventually, toward the end of our meal, two different groups got brave enough to come up to us. One was a couple and the other was a group of three, two young women and a guy who looked like college-aged friends.

Caleb introduced me to both of groups. He introduced me by my name, Stella Wilde, and didn't put any sort of label on me—friend or otherwise.

We were a few minutes early for the movie, and Caleb went to stand in line at the concession stand. I followed him over there even though I didn't normally get snacks at the movie. Once we found a spot in line, I turned to him and asked, "Are we getting something?"

"Of course," he said. "Why wouldn't we?"

I smiled. "Because we just ate."

"Yeah, but we didn't have dessert. You can't tell me you're trying to watch a movie without Milk Duds."

I laughed. "Milk Duds? Not popcorn or M&M's, even? Milk Duds?"

"Yeah, with the yellow box," he said, completely serious. "I was going to get popcorn, too," he added. "And a drink."

"You're partying too hard," I said, acting serious but being silly.

"I told you to watch out for me," he said, shrugging. We stepped up to the cashier just as he was saying that, and without hesitating, Caleb smiled and spoke to him.

"A small popcorn, a box of Milk Duds and whatever the lady wants to drink." He looked at me. "And whatever else you want to eat," he said. "If you want some other kind of candy or whatever."

I looked at the guy taking our order. "Milk Duds for me too, please. And an Icee."

"Coke or cherry?" the guy asked.

"Mixed."

Caleb shot me a glance. "Who's getting crazy now?" he said, causing me to laugh.

The guy working the counter told Caleb some ridiculous amount of money for a few snacks, and Caleb didn't bat an eye about paying it. I watched as he handed the guy some cash and waited for him to make change.

Caleb led me to the kiosk where we would find straws and napkins, and while we were over there, a friend of mine from college came up to me. We talked and caught-up for a minute while Caleb grabbed supplies.

I introduced Caleb by his first name, and didn't give him any sort of label the same way he had done for me. It was the thing that felt the most natural. I didn't want to call him a friend, but I didn't want to call him anything else.

I saw someone else I knew before we headed into the theater, and Caleb waved at one group, but we didn't talk to anyone else.

The theater was about half-full when we got there. We agreed on a place in the middle. The lights were on and people were talking, so we did the same. We ate bites of popcorn while talking about other movies we'd seen. Caleb remembered certain specific lines, and he was good at impressions. He made me laugh—and not just a fake laugh to humor him, but a genuine laugh. He was smart and disciplined but somehow funny and lighthearted at the same time. I loved his patience and attentiveness in conversation and the way his mind worked. I felt like my heart stopped every time I made eye contact with him. His dark eyes seemed bottomless when he was thinking, and I caught myself hoping it was me who was occupying his thoughts.

Caleb and I were not making eye contact at the moment. The previews were over and the movie was about to start. The audience was quiet, and I leaned in so that I could speak next to his ear. He was still looking at the screen, but he leaned toward me when he noticed what I was doing.

"May I have a couple of your candies?" I asked. "I just want one or two, and I hate to open mine."

Caleb held out the yellow box like he was going to pour some candy into my hand. I was holding the popcorn, so I balanced that bag in my right hand as I reached out with my left to take the candy.

Caleb used both hands. He reached under the backside of my hand, holding it steady as he poured. We had spent quite a bit of time together and rarely made any sort of physical contact. This contact was as close as we had ever come to holding hands. I tried to steady myself as the back of my hand rested in his big warm palm. His skin was slightly work-hardened and I loved the feel of it against mine. Caleb let the box of chocolate hover over my hand, hesitating there for a second before tilting it enough for a few candies to fall. I closed my hand around the candies, and slowly brought it back to my own lap so I could eat them.

Caleb leaned over to speak to me. I stretched that way, giving him my ear.

"You can have more candy anytime you want."

I nodded and pretended to be nonchalant.

I reached out again a moment or two later, and Caleb did that same maneuver where he unnecessarily held my hand to steady it while he poured candy.

The movie had started and it was quiet in the theater, so he wanted to cause as little distraction as possible. He pulled my hand near his chest and cradled it strategically, moving slowly and muffling any sound. He held it against his mid-section. I could feel the taut muscles in the area between his chest and stomach. He took even longer to get the candy into my hand that time. It was innocent, but he held my hand and I felt his body, and it caused my lungs to function at half capacity.

I did not even want the candy. I was full. But I ate it anyway, and it was so worth it. It was worth it enough that five or so minutes later, I held out my hand again, asking for more. Caleb took my hand like he was going to pour candy into it. I glanced over to watch him do it only to find that he was no longer holding the box of candy. It was resting upright in the cup holder that was on his other side.

He held my hand in his and he turned to glance at me when I looked that way. The lights from the movie screen flashed and moved, causing shadows to play on the side of his face.

"Did you really want candy?" he asked, speaking quietly. He was serious, and he stared at me, waiting for an answer. He had a hold of my hand, cradling it in front of him like he wasn't planning on letting me go. He was still waiting for me to answer his question. I had to tell him that I didn't care about the candy.

"No, I don't want candy," I said, staring at the screen as I leaned toward him.

Caleb held onto my hand. He was inexperienced but he was naturally bold, and it was with confidence that he held my hand gloriously captive.

For the remainder of that movie, Caleb held onto my hand. He wasn't just doing it casually or lightly, either. He gripped me with both of his hands, enveloping my hand and not letting me go.

Chapter 14

Caleb

He didn't want to let her go when the movie was over. He wanted to keep a hold of Stella Wilde for the rest of his life. At the moment, he felt like he didn't want to be out of her presence at all, ever again.

His emotions were so overwhelming that he decided to err on the side of discretion. He walked beside her on the way out of the theater but didn't make physical contact with her. It was difficult after holding her hand for so long in the theater. He had to fight against the urge to reach out and wrap his arm around her—to let everyone know who she was there with.

They were walking through the lobby when they got into a conversation that made Caleb regret not holding onto her.

"Heyyy Stella-umbrella!" a girl walked up to them, focusing her attention on Stella.

"Hey, Kate, what's going on?"

"Watching a movie," the girl said.

"Where's Collin?" Stella asked, hugging her friend.

"He had to stop and use the restroom. We just got done seeing that Russel Crowe movie."

"We saw that one, too," Stella said. "It was good."

"We're going to meet Nick and them at Jude's, after this" Kate said, looking around Stella curiously. "He said he was going out with you. Are you going there?"

Caleb's chest tightened. He was standing close to Stella, but he wasn't trying to intrude on their conversation. He had been trying to give her space to talk to her friend. Caleb had to resist the urge step forward and put his arm around her shoulders at the mention of those Nick and Jude characters, whoever they were. As if she could read his mind, Stella turned and gestured, acknowledging Caleb and stepping toward him.

"Kate this is Caleb. Caleb, my friend, Kate."

"Hello," Caleb said, reaching out to shake Kate's hand.

"Hi," Kate said. "How do you know Stella?"

"Her parents go to my church," Caleb said.

"And me. I go there too," Stella added. She looked at Caleb. "Kate and I go way back. We didn't go to high school together, but we knew each other back then from KCT."

"And we got closer in college," Kate added. She tilted her head as if in deep thought about something. "So, are both of you meeting Nick and them? Or are neither of you?"

"Neither," I said. "I wasn't planning on it. I talked to Nick earlier and told him I couldn't. He's meeting some of my friends from school. Other teachers. That's probably what he was talking about. They're my friends."

"Ah, okay, gotcha," Kate said. She hugged Stella.

"Okay, well you kids have fun," Stella said. "Tell everyone I said hi."

Stella seemed happy and content, and she was wearing what seemed to be a genuine smile as they began to walk away, but Caleb wondered if she felt like she was missing out. He did his best to keep calm even though he felt antsy and distracted. *Who was this Nick person and what was Stella doing talking to him earlier today? Why did Kate think Stella and Nick were going out tonight?* Caleb had to remind himself that Stella was not committed to him in any way and didn't owe him an explanation.

"I'm sorry," she said once they were out of earshot.

He held the door open for her, and she walked out ahead of him. "That probably sounded different than it was," she said as she walked past him.

"Oh, it's fine," Caleb said. "I was just thinking that you didn't owe me an explanation."

"Yeah, but thinking that must mean you also thought I *did* owe you one," Stella said.

Caleb contemplated that. It was true, and he smiled in reaction. "I wish you owed me one," he said.

"Nick's a friend," Stella replied. "He's a photographer. Nick Ferris. I had tentative plans to go out with some teacher friends of mine, girls, women, and they happen to be meeting him tonight. That was actually what I was talking about when you called earlier at school. That's when I said you helped me get out of something."

"I'm glad you didn't go," he said.

"I'm glad I didn't go, too," she said, bumping into him shyly as they walked.

He put his arm around her, and she leaned into him, responding. "Is there any way you could not go out with other guys, Stella?"

His question made her laugh, and that caused him to glance at her.

"What? Is that wrong of me to ask?" he asked.

"No, I just didn't expect you to ask it. I'm not dating anyone, if that's what you mean. Nick's definitely just my friend."

"No, that wasn't exactly what I meant," he said.

Stella's heart pounded and so did Caleb's, but both of them remained outwardly calm.

"I didn't plan on dating anyone so soon after everything that happened," she said.

Stella had told him the story of Liam while they were decorating the other night. She didn't mention Liam's name just now, but Caleb knew what she was referring to.

"What about tonight?" Caleb asked. "What do you think we're doing here? Do you think of this as a date?"

"Yeah, I would say so," she said with a nod. "I wanted it to be that."

They walked slowly in the parking lot, talking as they went. Caleb wanted to come right out and ask her to be his girlfriend. *Was that even what he would say to her?* He tried it out in his head, and it sounded extremely cheesy. *Would you be my girlfriend* seemed like a fifth-grade thing to ask, but he couldn't think of a better way to say it when that was what he wanted.

"Look, Stella, I know you went through a breakup and everything, but whenever you're ready to officially date someone, and not go out with anyone else, I would love for that person to be me. I just want to tell you that."

They had come to the passenger's side of his truck by then. "If it's going to be you, then I'm ready whenever, pretty much," she said. Stella was nervous and Caleb wasn't exactly sure what she had just said, but it seemed promising. Caleb stared at her, but she couldn't make eye contact with him. She stared at the pavement below her feet.

Caleb used a fingertip under her chin to urge her to look at him. Her skin was warm and so very soft. Her green eyes shimmered and shined even though it was dark out. He wondered how he had been given such a beautiful flower. Stella Wilde—his wild rose. He would never, ever take her for granted.

"Say that again," he said, staring at her. "Say what you just said."

She knew how he felt about her.

She could see it in his eyes.

"I am ready to date... but only if it's this one person. It's just this one guy I'd be interested in dating. No one else."

"Is his name Caleb?" Caleb asked.

"Yes," she answered.

"Is he me?" Caleb asked.

Stella's smile widened. It was so big, so genuine, that Caleb smiled and reached out to put his hand on her. He rested it on her back, pulling her slightly toward him. He felt like she was fragile, and he feared he might break her. Maybe it was just that whatever this was between them was so new and precious to him that it all seemed fragile. He wanted everything with this woman, but he knew he had to take it slower than that.

"He is you," Stella said, staring at him.

"Are you my girlfriend, Stella?"

She just stood there when he asked that. He could see by the way she blinked that she was holding back tears.

"Are you serious right now?" she asked with a nervous laughter that was meant to distract him from the tears of happiness that had formed in her eyes.

"I'm definitely serious," he said. "There's no other way to ask that except the cheesy way."

"I didn't think it was cheesy at all," she said.

It was cold out, and she shivered, drawing near to him. He held her closer, looking down at her. "It's cold out," he said. "Get in and we'll talk in the truck."

She nodded, and they went about the business of getting settled and starting the engine.

"Do you think people think I'm not good enough for you?" she asked once they were in their seats.

"Who would think that?" he asked.

"Lots of people."

"I don't think it," he said. "And I'm the only one who matters."

"What about your parents?" I asked.

"My parents trust my judgement. They've already heard that you and I have been on every available committee this week. They know I like you. They trust me to make a careful choice in the woman I date. That's good enough for them."

"I grew up in the church or whatever, Caleb, but for all intents and purposes, I'm a baby Christian."

"Baby Christians are Christians, too."

"I'm just trying to be honest with you. I searched *pastor's girlfriend*, and it said all sorts of stuff about being in a fishbowl or spotlight. Then I searched *pastor's wife* and these women come up who are pastors themselves. They speak at conferences and write Bible study books and stuff. I'm not... I can't

142

say for sure, but I don't see myself ever writing a book or speaking at a—"

"You don't need to be anyone but yourself, Stella." Caleb cut her off, but he smiled as he spoke. He shook his head at her, grinning.

"What?"

"You searched the internet."

"I did," she said. "But only after my brother acted shocked that I would like you. Or maybe he was shocked you would like me. I don't know which one confused him, honestly, but he didn't seem to think we were a match."

"Your brother, Tanner?" Caleb asked.

"Yes. I've probably done a few things in front of him, even recently, that I shouldn't have. I could see how he would think I wouldn't want to go out with the preacher or a preacher wouldn't want to go with me. I regret that I have to say any of this, but it's the truth, I thought you should know it."

"Is Tanner going to be disappointed if you start dating me?" he asked.

"No, no, definitely not. Tanner was just surprised, that's all, and it made me wonder if people would take issue with us, you know, dating."

"Some people take issue with just about anything," he said. "It's part of having any sort of platform. Ultimately, I have to decide what complaints are valid and worth listening to. I don't see why anyone would complain about me dating you, but if they do, I can say that I wouldn't listen."

"Then I won't listen either," Stella said.

Caleb put the truck in gear, but he looked at Stella before he backed out of the parking spot. "Do you have to get home right away, or can you go somewhere else with me?"

"I can definitely go somewhere," she said.

She was so quick to answer that he knew she'd go anywhere.

"Where is it?" she asked.

"How do you feel about playing the piano for me?"

"Where would I do that?"

"What about the church? There's that baby grand in the foyer for Christmas."

She agreed to it, and they pulled into the parking lot ten minutes later.

Chapter 15

Caleb

They went straight into the foyer when they arrived. Caleb unlocked the door and entered the alarm code. The enormous room was elongated and they had come in on the right-hand side of it. Caleb turned on a section of lights above them, but he left the lights in the other three sections of the room switched off. The Christmas tree was on the far side of the room near the piano, and Caleb knew it would make plenty of light once he turned it on. The two of them walked that way.

Thousands of tiny twinkling lights appeared all at once when he turned it on. There was a warm glow all around them.

"Ooh, we did good," Stella said staring up at the tree in its full glory.

"I know," he said. "I thought it would still be on when we got here. It runs at night because you can see it through the windows, but it's on a timer and it must have already turned off."

Stella went to the piano and sat on the bench. There were several seating areas in the foyer, and Caleb took a chair from the nearest one and turned it so that he could sit and watch her play rather than standing and staring over her shoulder.

Stella hit a few notes, testing the feel and sound of the piano.

"Clair de Lune," she announced quietly and with a nod.

Without any further ado, she started playing a song.

Caleb didn't know much about classical music, so he didn't know what to expect when she named the piece.

It was slow and measured, and she hit only a few notes at first. The combinations of notes were simple, delicate, beautiful. He had expected her to go off on something like *Flight of the Bumblebee*, and the slow thoughtful melody had him feeling gut-wrenched.

He felt like she was being vulnerable and he wanted to go to her, sit with her on the bench, hold her. The song sounded reflective, like it could have been on a movie soundtrack.

Her fingers expertly roamed over the keys, hitting simple sequences of notes with flawless pace and accentuation. Caleb was so mesmerized by the sound of the music that he stared into space at a random spot on the keys of the piano.

It was actually unbelievable to him that Stella could do this. His flower, his prize, his lady, the woman who had already won his heart, turned out to be a living, breathing music box. She touched the keys with an expert grace that indicated years upon years of practice.

146

He hadn't been around her for any of that.

God had been making and molding her into the woman Caleb needed and wanted. He thought about the attributes he had asked God for in a wife, and never once had he mentioned wanting a musician. God knew him better than he knew himself.

Tears came to his eyes at the gratitude he felt. He watched her with blurred vision, feeling humbled and undeserving of such a sweet gift. The music was perfect. The piece she played was dramatic and the sound of it added to Caleb's overwhelming sense of pride and gratefulness.

She hit some low notes, and the sound vibrated in his chest. She sat upright with perfect posture and poise. She was so funny and easy to get along with that her patient sense of timing and grace at the piano were unexpected to him.

It was extremely difficult for Caleb to keep it together as he watched her play. The only reason he didn't bury his face in his hands and weep was that he was too afraid to miss it. He watched, mesmerized, eyes stinging, as she played.

The song was over too soon.

Stella stopped playing and took a deep breath, and then she swiveled on the bench, her eyes meeting his. Stella could see the tears in his eyes combined with his stunned expression, and she stood up and crossed to him instantly.

She didn't hesitate or ask permission. She just took a seat on his leg, sitting upright just like she had been on the piano bench. Caleb's chest was so tight it felt like it might explode. He wanted to be married to her already. He took a deep breath. He was rigid underneath Stella, reigning in his emotion and attraction.

"Did you like it?" she asked.

"I... can't... think of anything I could have liked more than that," he said dazedly. Caleb stared into her eyes, and she blinked and smiled. He couldn't believe she actually thought she might not be good enough for him. That seemed ludicrous. She was perfect. He felt so much love and attraction that he found himself wanting to get some form of commitment from her right then.

"Do you know you're my girlfriend?"

His question made her giggle. "Yes," she said. She put her hands on the sides of his face. They were the same hands that had made those sounds come out of the piano, and the thought of it caused Caleb to experience all sorts of urges.

Then she kissed him.

She was sitting on his lap, and her face was slightly above his. She leaned down, hands on his cheeks, and kissed him—right on the lips. Her soft mouth touched his, and Caleb held his breath.

He felt like he could jump out of his own skin.

She kissed him gently. She did it twice on the lips, and then she pulled back and kissed his cheek and then his mouth again.

"Guess what, Caleb?" she asked.

"What, Stella?" he asked, barely breathing.

The corner of her mouth rose in a sideways grin. "I'm your girlfriend," she said. She was a little shy about it, and she bit her lip.

He wrapped his arms around her waist, holding her in place. "I knew you could play," he said. "And I figured you could play well. I tried to prepare myself for that—picture it. I tried to imagine what it would be like when I got to hear you. But I wasn't quite prepared, Stella. Seeing you, and the sound of it. I feel a little undeserving at the moment."

"Stop," she said as if she thought he might be teasing.

"I'm serious. I didn't expect you to be able to do that. I can't imagine how many hours you had to practice to make it sound like that. I can't believe God would... anyway, I do feel undeserving."

"Well, I feel undeserving with you, too, Caleb. Look at all this," she said glancing around them. "You have all this to take care of... all these people to lead. I don't know how to fit into this world." Her eyes met his again. She touched his cheeks with her fingertips. "What I'm saying is that there's no sense in both of us feeling undeserving. It'd probably be best if neither of us did."

"How'd you get to be so smart?" he asked, speaking quietly, staring at her.

She shrugged.

"Come here and let me show you something," he said.

Caleb patted Stella's legs like he wanted her to stand up, and she did. He grabbed her by the hand and walked with her into a door on the backside of the foyer. Most of the doors off of the foyer led to the main auditorium, but this wasn't one of them. They ended up in a hallway that would eventually take them around the side of the church to the offices.

"Where are we going?" she asked. He didn't answer. He just kept walking until he got to a nook that was jutting off of the right side of the hallway. It was a little seating area with a loveseat, two chairs, and a coffee table. Caleb sat on the couch and pulled her onto his lap. She hadn't been expecting that, and she laughed as she landed there.

"What are you doing?" she asked, smiling at him.

"Getting back to how we were," he said.

Caleb held her much more securely now than he had been in the foyer. He was bear-hugging her so tightly that she giggled and squirmed.

"Why did we move?" Stella asked, adjusting in his arms.

"Why do you think?" he said.

She glanced around, searching for clues.

"Because someone could have seen us through the windows?" she asked.

"Yeah, I guess that too, but also the cameras. There are several in the foyer."

"Oh dang."

"Why oh dang? he asked.

"Because I sat on your lap," she said, making a worried expression. "I shouldn't have done that. I didn't even think about cameras."

He squeezed her. "You don't need to worry about the cameras, and you should have done it. I'm happy you sat on my lap. That was where I wanted you to sit. I don't care about anyone seeing you doing that, I just didn't want to share with anybody what happens next."

"What is it?" she asked. "What's happening next?"

"What do you think?"

"Are you maybe gonna try to kiss me again?" she asked.

The suggestion—the sound of that word coming off of her lips made Caleb feel so affected that he didn't answer her right away. His hesitation made her just nervous enough to keep talking.

"I bet you're an expert at kissing girls at church. You probably know all the nooks and crannies where there are no cameras."

"Yeah, I bring women in here and kiss them all the time," he said. "I kiss women left and right while I'm up here." He was clearly being sarcastic, but Stella narrowed her eyes and made a face like she didn't want to hear that.

Caleb smiled at her jealous smirk.

He couldn't hold out any longer.

He pulled her closer while at the same time leaning toward her. She leaned in and their lips came together. Caleb stopped moving when they were only an inch or two from making contact. He stared at her. He had already felt her lips on his, but he hadn't yet kissed her the way he wanted to. He ached to do it. He had been fighting against the urge all evening.

"I have never in my life kissed a woman in a church," he said quietly, trying to seem more level-headed than he was.

"Never?" she asked, looking like she didn't quite believe it.

"Never."

"Not in this specific church?" she asked, knowing he'd been in England for nearly a decade.

"Not in any church," he said.

He spoke slowly with his mouth torturously close to hers. He held onto her, his big carpenter arms wrapped securely around her waist.

He wanted her to be his forever.

He knew she would be.

He wondered if she knew it too.

He kissed her.

He leaned in, opening his mouth the instant they made contact. He took her bottom lip into his, and her hands came up, touching the sides of his face, pulling him near like she had done in the foyer. She let out a little whimper at the feel of his open-mouthed kiss, and Caleb knew it was permission for him to deepen it.

He yielded somewhat to his own desire. He was still in control and he knew he wouldn't let things go too far, but he kissed Stella Wilde differently that night. He kissed her the way a man kisses the woman he desires. Caleb's desire was built on love and patience, and he controlled every second of the kiss, never letting it go too far. It was passionate, but it was also slow, sweet, and warm.

He thought Stella was perhaps the most beautiful, lovely woman on the whole face of the earth. He would rather be with her than anyone else. He could not wait to marry her.

Chapter 16

Stella

It was after midnight when Caleb and I finally left that couch in the hallway. He held me there, talking to me and kissing me gently for hours. I sat on his lap for some of the time, and then I moved to sit next to him, but he never stopped holding me. His arms stayed blissfully wrapped around me. Caleb's solid, steady embrace was perhaps the best physical location I had ever experienced.

He loved it when I called myself his girlfriend. A few times, while we were sitting there, I said the phrase and he always grinned and kissed me for it.

Neither of us looked at our phones the whole time we were sitting there—not even to check the time. It wasn't until we got into his truck and I saw the clock on the dashboard that I noticed how late it was.

"Whoa, we were there a long time."

"I know," he said. "I didn't realize."

Once we got on the road, he stretched his hand onto the console, and I reached out to hold it with no hesitation. I wasn't even a hundred percent sure he was holding it out there for me to take, but I took it. I brought his hand closer to me and held it up to my face, rubbing the backside of it on my cheek.

"I should probably go to Tanner's basketball game tomorrow," he said.

"Yeah, I guess so," I said. "Since my dad invited you."

"Do we do this in front of other people?" he asked, referring to the way I carefully cradled his hand.

"Not exactly like this," I answered, smiling. "I can't see myself sitting there and rubbing your hand on my cheek at the basketball game." We both laughed a little and I added, "But regular hand-holding is probably okay if you ever have the urge to do that. If you want that. We don't have to. There will be a lot of people there—some of whom I know for sure go to your church, so I would understand if you—"

I stopped talking in mid-sentence because Caleb had pulled my hand to his lap and brought the back of it to his mouth. I watched it happen and felt a crippling wave of desire as I saw his mouth touch my skin. He was telling me that I didn't need to talk about future plans for hand-holding. He was telling me that we were on the same page about it—that we would do it and not care what anyone thought.

"It starts at two o'clock," I said. "I can't remember if my dad said it was at Dunbar or not. It'll be in town either way."

"Just let me know, and I'll meet you there."

"Oh, I was thinking you would ride with us," I said.

155

"Okay," he agreed. "I'm doing some work at my parents' in the morning, but I'll wrap it up so that I can be at your house by one. Will that be enough time?"

I nodded. "My parents might leave early to catch some of the JV game. But you and I can leave at whatever time and meet them."

***

Caleb went with me to that basketball game.

He held my hand, too.

In fact, in the days that followed, he went to almost every basketball game with me, and he held onto me all the time.

Caleb was instantly and wholly devoted. He was a no-nonsense drama-free boyfriend. He somehow managed to show me PDA all the time while never seeming improper or making people uncomfortable. He was a gentleman's gentleman—a solid rock of a man who was reasonable and kind and physically gorgeous.

We both worked full-time, but I consolidated my piano lessons to two afternoons a week so that most of my afternoons and evenings were free. Caleb and I stayed busy every night for the next couple of weeks. We spent a ton of time together, getting to know each other and our families.

Despite the fact that he grew up in Lexington, Caleb didn't know much about horses. My brother, Justin, along with my cousins and uncle, were experts, and Caleb always enjoyed talking to them and learning more about breeding, training, and racing horses.

We got along great with each other's families, but we loved being alone, too. He and I had conversations that were deep and intimate and lasted for hours. Early on, I came to the conclusion that Caleb was simply a good person, and he constantly lived up to that. He put God first in such a way that his life just sort of effortlessly centered around Him. But in spite of Caleb's occupation and his love for the Lord, he did not come across as overly religious. He was funny and approachable and everyone was drawn to him—even those who weren't ready to have God in their life at that moment.

He got along with everyone. I could see Caleb gently and discreetly planting God's seeds in people's lives. He was a natural at building people up. He would say true, poignant, encouraging words in conversation. I could see people's countenance change as they talked to him.

Tanner's coach caught on to Caleb's abilities and he started asking him to say a prayer for the team before the game. Several times, he had gone into the locker room before the team came out.

Caleb was straight as an arrow—as solid and upstanding as they came. He was so good and right that I felt like I had no choice but to throw myself wholeheartedly into the relationship. I would be good to Caleb and I would work to keep him by my side and make him happy.

He was, no doubt, a hundred percent, the one I wanted on my team. He was nothing like any other man I had ever dated. Technically, maybe he wasn't the type of man I was normally drawn to, but now that I was with him, I knew he was exactly my type. He was so right for me that it was almost as if I had been lying to myself about what I liked in a man my whole life.

Either way, I was wholly devoted and so was he. Caleb Gray and I were joined at the hip. We shifted our schedules and made time to be together anytime we weren't working. We definitely factored into each other's Christmas plans this year.

In the weeks leading up to Christmas, Caleb and I had several houses to visit and parties to attend. We had already gone to a few of them. It was currently the evening of the 23rd, and tonight we were having the big Christmas party at his parents' house.

This wasn't to be confused with the small, intimate celebration we would have with his parents, Josiah, and a few others on Christmas Day. This was the gathering with uncles and aunts and cousins and friends. This was the big one—the one my own parents and siblings were going to this year. The Grays had insisted that we invite my family. I mentioned it to them thinking they would decline or say they had something else going on, but they agreed to come. My brother, Justin, and his wife were coming and so were my parents and Tanner. It was a huge party with at least a hundred people.

Caleb and I got there early, and there were already several cars in the driveway. Caleb said by the time the party began, cars would be parked all the way down the street.

He was right. People just kept coming through the door. It would definitely be the largest party we went to this year. I had a pretty big family on both my mother and father's side, but neither of those Christmas get-togethers were as large as this one.

The Gray's had a lovely home. It was stately, but it wasn't an absolute mansion like the one where Uncle Ezekiel lived. It was a large home, but with all of those people there, we were certainly in close quarters.

We were at the party for two hours and had already eaten when Caleb asked me if I wanted to step outside onto the back patio. There was a gas fireplace in the center of a large seating area and there were also four outdoor heaters positioned strategically around the perimeter of the patio. Temperature was bearable, but it was definitely cool, even with the heaters.

It was for this reason that the outdoor area was not packed. There were people sitting on couches and in chairs, maybe ten or twelve total, but it was far fewer than there were inside. They were all engaged in their own conversations.

I had been inside talking with a big group when Caleb told me to meet him out there. He went to the restroom on our way, saying he would meet me on the patio in just a minute.

He must have not stopped to talk to anyone because I had only been waiting a minute or two when he joined me. I smiled as he crossed the patio, heading my way. He walked past a few people, but his eyes were trained on me and he came to me quickly.

His smile was irresistible, and it gave me that yearning feeling in the pit of my stomach that almost made me want to giggle as I waited for him to approach. I couldn't be prouder of him. I loved his family, and I felt like all was right with the world. He came up and turned me in his arms, holding me with my back to his chest. We were both facing the fire, and Caleb lowered his head to speak near my ear.

"I love you," he said.

I squeezed his arms, holding him in place as he held me. It wasn't the first time he had said that to me, but it was still new enough that it gave me all sorts of feelings—ooey gooey feelings.

"I love you too," I said, whispering shyly and squirming a little. He smelled good, and people weren't paying much attention to us, so I pressed my face into his chest and neck.

"Stella." There was a serious edge to his tone that caused me to straighten and pay attention. I shifted slightly in his arms, turning and waiting to hear what he would say when he continued. "I'm going to take you by the hand in just a second, and we'll go inside. Once we're in there, I'm going to make a little speech. It'll just be minute or two. But at the end of it I'm going to ask you to marry me, okay? Could you please just say yes to that question when I ask it?"

"Yes, I will. Of course I will."

The words came out right away, but my voice sounded choked. My heart was suddenly in my throat.

"I can't b-believe all these—do these people know you're going to—"

I didn't even finish the question because Caleb was nodding. "I can't believe you didn't catch on," he said. "Uncle Aaron was dropping hints left and right."

I smiled thoughtfully, remembering his Uncle Aaron. "I just thought he was weird," I said, causing Caleb to laugh.

"He is weird."

"I was also wondering why my whole family was here," I said as things began to sink in.

He shrugged a little. "They would have been invited anyway. They'll be invited next year if they want to come."

I smiled at the fact that he was talking about the future. "It sounds like you already know what my answer will be," I said.

161

"I hope I know," he said.

"You do know."

"I love you," he said. "This is going to be fun."

"What is?" I asked. "This moment, or forever?"

"Both, for sure," he said. "Everything's going to be fun from here on out."

"Thank you for warning me," I said.

I didn't necessarily want to cry in front of everyone, and I felt like if he sprang this on me, I wouldn't be able to enjoy it as much.

"Are you ready now that you've been warned?" he asked with a confident grin.

I nodded and he gave me a little squeeze before ushering me back into the house.

Chapter 17

Caleb was extremely comfortable with public speaking. He effortlessly held all of our attention. He frequently smiled when he was talking, and that made him seem approachable. One of the main things that made him an engaging speaker was that he was passionate about his subject matter. Normally it was Jesus, but tonight it was me, and after all the things he said, there was no doubt in any of our minds that he loved me.

He said things like, *"God told me I would meet the woman I would marry when I came back home. I didn't know how long it would take or who it would be, but I knew it was going to happen. And I knew Stella was the one the very instant I laid eyes on her."* He also said things like, *"This might seem quick to some of you, but from where I stand, I've been waiting my whole life for it."*

Caleb told stories, highlighting a few things I didn't even know he remembered. He talked about a couple of interactions we had when we were younger—ones that he hadn't mentioned to me before tonight.

I cried. I had been warned that it was coming, but his speech was just too much. It was overwhelming. There was nothing off-the-cuff about it. The things he said were all very planned and rehearsed. He made it seem like he was thinking of it all on the spot, but he wasn't. I knew him and I knew how much effort and planning went into his preparation and delivery. It was perfect. He made everyone laugh and he was sincere and simple.

At the end of it all, he got down on his knee and asked me to please marry him. I, of course, said yes. There was cheering and hugging and patting of backs. It was all a big whirlwind.

What added to it was that I had no idea he was going to ask me that night—even with my family being there and his uncle acting a little weird, I still didn't put it together.

Caleb's life was very much in the spotlight, and I thought for propriety's sake he would end up dating me for a long while before asking me to marry him. I didn't expect him to do it that evening, but I also didn't hesitate to agree to marry him when he asked.

He was a hundred percent correct when he said it might seem quick to others, but it was natural to us. I certainly didn't see a reason to waste any time. I couldn't imagine loving anyone else like I loved Caleb. I knew spending my life with him was the right thing to do.

He proposed to me on the twenty-third, and for the next couple of days, at Christmas celebrations, we recounted the story to friends and family who hadn't been there. Neither of us did too much social media, so there hadn't been an official announcement from us, but people had been there and taken pictures with us for their own social media, and that was how the news of our engagement got out. I got texts and comments and calls from people who had heard through the grapevine, so I knew it was being talked about. Caleb chose a beautiful ring, and his cousin had me flash it in a photo she took of us on the first night, so a lot of random people saw it the day it happened.

It didn't surprise me that Liam found out about it, but it honestly surprised me that he cared. I hadn't heard a thing from him at all since he moved, and then I get engaged and three days later he showed up on my doorstep.

It was the day after Christmas, and I had slept in before helping my mom fold laundry and then deciding to chip away at some of my lesson planning for school. Caleb was working on a carpentry project—one for me, actually, a bookshelf. He would not finish up until later in the afternoon.

It was early afternoon, and I was still in my lounge-around clothes when Liam came over.

I was sitting at my father's desk doing some lesson planning when my mother came into the room wearing a deer in the headlights expression.

"He came by. He's here. He asked if he could please come in and talk to you, and I didn't know what to say. He just kind of invited himself in."

"Who?" I asked, sitting up straight.

"Liam," Mom said, almost whispering.

She cut her eyes to the side as if indicating that he was right around the corner.

"He's in here? Why'd you let him in?"

"Is he dangerous or something?" she asked, looking suddenly very concerned.

"No... but still," I said. "Where is he?"

"In the living room."

"You invited him in?"

She shrugged. "I told you, he just came up and asked if he could please come inside and talk to you. I didn't know what to say. I didn't know he was coming over, so I just opened the door. I thought it was the UPS guy."

I sighed as I stood up. I dreaded seeing Liam. The thought of it caused me to feel nauseated. I wanted to ask my mother to walk back out there and tell him to leave, but it wasn't her mess to clean up.

"Should I go with you?" she asked, a little concerned.

I shook my head. "No. Please don't actually. It's already embarrassing enough as it is having to talk to him here. I'm not going anywhere else with him, though."

She nodded. "I'll leave you alone," Mom said. "And dad won't be back for another hour or two. But you better yell if you need anything."

I smiled. "He's not a threat. I'm not scared. I just don't feel like seeing him."

"I'll stay back here. I could use this time to strip the sheets. You can talk to him out there."

She parted ways with me in the hallway, me headed to the living room, and Mom headed to her bedroom.

My gut twisted and a wave of dread washed over me as I walked that way. I did not even care that I was basically still in my pajamas and had no makeup on. I had no desire to impress him.

I felt relief and fear at the same time when I rounded the corner and saw his familiar face staring back at me. He was striking and mysterious looking in a rockstar type of way. He wore mostly black, and I used to think he was the hottest thing ever. *What had I been thinking?* He was small and slithery compared to Caleb. He smiled warmly and stepped toward me as I walked his way.

"Hey," I said, stopping ten or so feet from him and staring at him curiously. "What's up?"

"Hey," he said, cautiously.

He gestured toward the couch. "Could we please sit and catch up for a second?"

I wanted to say that I was in the middle of work, which was the truth. But then I would be putting this little meeting off and would only dread it happening in the future. I knew it was better to get it over with, so that was what I decided to do. I rounded the edge of the couch, sticking right next to the couch as I moved stiffly. I took a seat on the opposite end, staying as far from him as possible without making it overly obvious that I was avoiding him.

I found a spot on the edge of the couch, unable to act comfortable and relaxed. I glanced in his direction when he didn't speak right away.

"How have you been?" he asked.

His tone was careful.

Did he feel sorry for me?

Then I remembered my appearance and I put it together that he must think something was wrong with me if I was still loafing around the house in the middle of the afternoon.

"It's the day after Christmas," I explained. "And I was back there working."

"How's work going?" he asked.

"Better," I said, honestly.

It had gotten better. Maybe it helped that my perspective had changed. I was more lighthearted about it and didn't stress so much since I had met Caleb. It wasn't just about being with him, either. He was teaching me how to trust God with things I couldn't control and concentrate on the things I could. I was simply happier as a person. I did not desire Liam at all or feel like I was missing anything not being with him.

"I told you it would get better if you hung in there," Liam said. I just smiled thoughtfully and nodded since I wanted to get the conversation over with.

He swiveled in his seat and ducked, trying to get me to look at him. I glanced that way with a cautious smile.

"I'm so sorry," he said. "I'm sorry for how things... it was terrible for me, leaving you, Stella."

"You don't need to say that," I said, doing my best to remain calm and unaffected.

"I came here to tell you I'm sorry," he said. "I should have been more sensitive about everything. This is all my fault."

"It's fine, really," I said, meaning it.

"No, it's not," he said, shaking his head and looking regretful, sorrowful.

"It is. Really."

"I heard you were getting married," he said, looking so focused and serious that I made a curious expression.

"I am," I said, wondering what was the matter with him.

He shook his head, looking downcast. "Collin said it was to some preacher."

"He's not just *some preacher*, but I don't really need to clarify that with you."

"You can't possibly actually like him," Liam said.

I let out an uncontrollable scoff. "What's that mean? Of course I like him. I love him."

Liam stared deep into my eyes, looking seriously concerned like I was on the verge of having a nervous breakdown or doing something to hurt myself. "Stella, please." His tone was pleading, somber.

"Please what, Liam?" I asked.

"Please don't do this to yourself."

He put his hands out as if trying to reason with me. But I just looked to him with an expression that said I thought he was the crazy one.

"Stella. I feel responsible for this. That's why I'm here. I need you to try to see yourself from the outside. Just a few months ago, you and I were living together, and now you're engaged to someone else. Not only that, Stella, but you're supposed to be marrying a preacher. Imagine how I felt when I heard that."

"So what if he's a preacher, Liam?"

"So a lot of things, and Stella."

He reached toward me trying to touch my knee. He said the word "Baby," to preface whatever he was going to say next, but I spoke at the same time.

"Don't," I said, pulling my leg away so that he couldn't touch me.

"Listen. I just want to talk to the old Stella for a second," Liam said quietly, trying to be reasonable.

"You are talking to her," I said, matter-of-fact.

He shook his head sadly. "The old Stella would not get herself into something like this."

"Something like what?"

"A preacher, Stella? And someone you just met? This has desperation written all over it. Depression."

I put a hand to my chest instantly. "You think *I'm* depressed?" I asked, letting out a little uncontrollable laugh.

"Stella, baby, please try to reason with me. I know you're stronger than this."

It was the second time he called me baby. I had ignored the first, but not this one.

"First, I'm not baby to you, and second, Liam, I'm definitely strong. My strength is not in question here. I'm stronger than ever. You have nothing to worry about."

I continued to stare at him like he was the one who was confused, since he was.

Liam let out a dramatic sigh. "Stella, if you could just see yourself from our perspective. If you could take in this situation from the outside, you would appreciate how crazy it is."

I stared at him, not knowing how in the world to respond to that.

Chapter 18

"Liam, no offense, but you have no idea what you're talking about," I said, shaking my head a little and feeling stunned.

"I know that a few months ago, you didn't even know this guy Stella. I know that you'd never, in a million years, marry a preacher. That's just... I'm sorry, but I still care enough about you to not let you do this to yourself." He paused and cut his eyes toward the hallway. "I honestly don't understand how your parents are letting this happen. Do they know about it?"

"Of course they know about it," I said. "They were there when he proposed. They celebrated with us."

I made that last statement with a concerned expression. If he could look at me like he was questioning my sanity, then I could do the same thing to him.

"Stella, I'm just here to help. I wish you could see that. I care about you. I don't want to see you do this to yourself."

I was speechless. I felt angry with him for belittling what I had with Caleb, but I did my best to stay calm and not get emotional because I knew that would only make it seem like he was right.

"Thank you, Liam, but I don't need help. I'm better off now than I've ever been. I'm happy. So happy. Thank you, but there's absolutely nothing for you to be concerned about."

"You can't tell me you're actually going to marry this guy," he said.

"You can't tell me you actually care," I returned.

"I don't care. I mean, not like that. I-I'm not trying to... I didn't... I'm not j-just trying to come here and break you up."

"I'm sorry, I must be confused. Why are you here, then?"

"I'm here for you, Stella. I'm not saying we have to get back together. I'm still in Boston, and I'm... I'm just... I'm here for you right now, Stella. I don't want to see you go off the deep end because of something I did. You deserve better than that. I feel like I need to make things right with you."

It was infuriating to me that he actually thought he was doing me a favor right now. I wanted to explode on him, and I had to pray to keep from doing so. I took a deep, measured breath.

"I wasn't expecting to meet Caleb, Liam. I didn't go out searching for a relationship, and I didn't jump into anything. I'm ready for this, and I want it. I am happy, content, strong, healthy, calm, confident, and sure of myself. I don't know how else to say it, Liam, but I am in the exact situation I want to be in. There is nothing depressed or desperate about how I feel. My decision to marry Caleb was made with gratefulness and happiness. I'm not out of my mind.

The opposite is true. There's no need for you to worry, I promise."

I smiled and spoke with such calm certainty that I could see that things were finally sinking in for him. He didn't seem convinced that I was making the right choice necessarily, but he could see that I was sure of myself and not going to budge on the subject.

I got to my feet the instant I saw his expression shift.

"Well, I'm glad we got that cleared up," I said. "Good talk. Thank you, Liam, for caring enough to stop by." I gave him a patient smile. "It means a lot. But I promise I'm good. I'm happy. I hope you are too."

Liam got to his feet. He looked introspective, like things weren't quite settled from his point of view.

"I'm happy," he said, nodding a little.

"Are things going good for you in Boston?" I asked. I began heading toward the door, walking as we talked.

"They are. I sold that sunflower piece."

"Really?" I asked. "To who?"

"This couple. They bought that crow piece and then came back for it a week later."

"Did you do okay on it?" I asked, knowing he was trying to get ten-thousand for it.

"They didn't ask me to come down," he said.

"Oh, that's great," I said. I really meant it and it came out sounding that way. I didn't have ill-feelings toward Liam. I was so happy with my life now that I didn't begrudge anything it took to get me to that place.

We walked toward the door, and I stopped when we got there since I wasn't about to walk him out.

"You seem so distant," Liam said.

"I'm sorry," I said. "I don't mean to be. I didn't expect you to come over."

"I haven't stopped thinking about you since I heard you were getting married the other night."

"You could have just texted me and asked me if I was okay," I said. "You didn't have to come all the way from Boston just to have this conversation."

"W-well, I was, uh, I was visiting for the holidays, and I—"

"I know, Liam, I'm just messing with you. I know you came in to visit Jo and Hank." (Jo and Hank were his mom and stepdad.) I was much calmer than Liam was, and he seemed confused by it. "Seriously, though," I said, opening the door to let him walk out. "Thanks for checking on me. That was kind of you."

He stepped across the threshold, staring at me with a completely unreadable expression. He was definitely confused, but I didn't feel like analyzing his feelings beyond that.

"Please call me if you ever need anything," he said. "Anything at all, Stella."

I could have explained that I would never need to call him, but honestly it wasn't worth my time. I just smiled and nodded. "Thank you," I said. "You're awesome."

My words were kind enough to mask the fact that I was basically shoving him out the door.

"Good job with selling that sunflower painting. Congratulations on that," I said, laying it on thick as he stepped outside. He stopped on the front stoop when he saw that I was not going to follow him. I waved as I slowly closed the door behind him.

"Bye, Liam. Thanks again, and Happy New Year!"

I smiled brightly until the door was completely closed, at which time I let my face fall and my shoulders drop. I turned and leaned my back against the door.

Oh, my goodness, what in the world? The audacity of him to think he was rescuing me, helping me. And the funny part was that he didn't even do it because he wanted to be with me—that made it even more offensive.

I cringed at the memory of his expression. He seriously pitied me, which was insane. It had not been a fun conversation, but I thought I had done a good job of remaining confident and in control in spite of my emotions. I was still standing there thinking about the whole thing a couple of minutes later when my mother came down the hall.

"Are you okay?" she asked. "I was watching the driveway from my room. I just saw him pull out."

"Yeah, he just left," I said.

"What was that all about?"

She crossed to the kitchen and began absentmindedly wiping the counter, so I walked that way, joining her in there.

I cried tears of frustration.

I tried not to start, but there was nothing I could do to stop myself. I had been solid as a rock while Liam was there, but I couldn't hold out any longer.

"Stella, are you... what happened?"

She was obviously concerned, and I shook my head and waved my mom off even though tears were actively flowing.

"I'm okay," I said, although I had to speak slowly and through tears. "I am. It's all fine. I'm just frustrated. Embarrassed, mostly. Mad, maybe." I hated that I was crying when I wasn't even sad. I begged myself to stop. "I'm not sad," I clarified. "I'm... I don't know. I'm just... I hope no one thinks Caleb and me are crazy for getting engaged so quick. I just worry about him. I'm not worried about myself. Liam was saying all this about it seeming crazy from the outside—you know—us getting engaged so quick."

"He's probably just jealous and making you feel bad. He probably sees what he's missing out on now that you're with someone else. I'm sure he heard about it."

"He did hear about it. That's why he came. But he wasn't jealous. He just came to confront me because he thought I went crazy."

"That's just silly," Mom said.

"I know it is. But it makes me worry that other people feel that way too. I mean, maybe if we were going to stay engaged for a long time it wouldn't matter, but Caleb's talking about getting married soon."

"How soon?" Mom didn't mean to do it, but her surprise made me feel even worse.

I let out a little hopeless laugh. "I don't know," I said. The truth was that Caleb had already said he wanted to do it as soon as possible. He said he would go to the courthouse with me if I agreed.

I hated that other people had opinions about what we did with our lives. I also hated that I cared what those opinions were. That thought made me cry even more. I buried my face in my hands.

"It's really not a big deal," I said, through burning tears that I knew would stop any second. "I'm just mad at him for coming. I wasn't expecting him. That was the last thing I expected to deal with today." I thought of meeting him in my pajamas with no makeup. "I'm going to take a shower," I said resolutely.

"Is Caleb still coming over for dinner?" Mom asked.

I nodded. "He's working on my bookcase. He'll be here in about an hour. We're going to take Elmo for a walk."

Elmo was my father's terrier dog. He was mostly an outside pet. He had a nice bed in the garage, and he stayed in there when temperatures were extreme, but he spent a lot of time outside. He never came all the way into the house. He had a good life, though. My dad had a little shop out in the garage, and he spent a lot of time out there.

Caleb and I took Elmo on walks for our own enjoyment. Caleb often talked about getting a dog. He had wanted one ever since he had been living on his own and he never felt settled enough to do it. We had already talked about taking him to the park that evening.

"Isn't it too cold?" Mom asked. She always asked that, and we always told her we'd bundle up.

"No ma'am," I said. "We'll dress warm. I'm gonna hop in the shower and get ready."

Chapter 19

I quit crying by the time I got in the shower. It wasn't a specific thought or sequence of thoughts that made me stop. I knew it had just been a burst of frustrated tears, anyway.

I let cool water hit my face, hoping it would soothe any puffiness. My face was hot, and the contrasting temperature of the water felt amazing.

I didn't know what to think about Liam's visit. Honestly, I felt sorry for him that he was wasting his time worrying about me. In actuality, I was the one who pitied him. It was unbelievable that he thought I needed an intervention when I was the one who was finally feeling happy and content—fulfilled. I was the one who was blind but now could see, and *he was feeling sorry for me?*

It was frustrating, but I did my best not to give it too much of my time and energy. My thoughts drifted to Liam and our interaction as I got dressed, but it wasn't to the point that I couldn't function or think of other things.

Ultimately, I knew the extent of my feelings for Caleb, and I took comfort that there was no doubt or regret whatsoever as a result of seeing Liam. As an inadvertent result of my annoyance, I took more time than usual get dressed. I put on some makeup and I wore my best skinny jeans and a sweater. I even took time drying and styling my hair. Maybe it was a lot of effort for an evening at the park, but it felt good to feel prepared to see Caleb.

I saw him pull up and I walked outside to meet him. He stepped out of his truck, smiling at me.

Caleb.

He was a sight for sore eyes—so much more substantial and solid than Liam. He was dressed warm, wearing jeans and a long sleeve shirt layered over a t-shirt. He was also wearing a coat. He looked sharp and handsome. I knew he had just taken a shower because his hair was still a little damp.

I was so proud of him and happy to see him.

I grinned as I walked straight into his arms. He saw what I was doing and opened his arms, hugging me, holding me. He had definitely just taken a shower. His shower gel was familiar to me, and I recognized it as soon as my face was resting near chest.

"Hello to you, too," he said, a smile in his tone. His deep voice resonated in his chest and I smiled at the sound of it.

"I missed you," I said.

"I missed you too," he said. "I was making you something. You're going to love it."

"I know I will. You're gonna get cold on a walk with your hair wet," I said even though my face was still resting on his chest and I wasn't even looking at his hair.

"I thought we were heading into the house," he said. "Did you want to go to the park right now? I have a beanie in the truck."

"We can, but we don't have to. I was just... Mom's in the house, and I thought we could hang out, just the two of us—maybe stay outside for a minute."

Caleb shifted as he pulled back a little to peer down at me. "Are you okay?" he asked, knowing a little something was off.

"Yeah. I'm just... so, so, so glad you're here." We were close to his truck, so he broke contact with me just long enough to open the door and grab his knitted navy-blue beanie. I watched as he quickly pulled it onto his head before smiling at me and opening his arms again. He was a hat guy. I had seen him wear this hat before, and he looked irresistible in it. I went into his arms, leaning back and looking straight up at him.

"Why are you so, so, so glad instead of just regular glad?" he asked, teasing me, holding me by my waist.

"Because..."

I trailed off for a second, thinking. It crossed my mind that it would be awkward to hold out any longer on telling him the truth about my unexpected visitor. I said it. I went ahead and admitted the truth. I probably should have thought more about how I would approach it, but I ended up just blurting it out.

"Liam came over," I said.

Caleb's face instantly went from neutral/happy to curious/irritated.

"When?" he asked.

"Earlier."

"Today?"

I nodded.

"Did you ask him to?" he asked, seeming a little confused.

"No. Of course not. I didn't want him here."

"Were you by yourself? Why didn't you call me? I was just at my dad's. I would have dropped everything and—"

"I didn't need you to drop everything and come," I said, interrupting him. "I was fine. I'm just glad you're here now."

I held onto Caleb's waist. His muscles were tight. I could feel how solid he was even underneath the layers of clothing. He looked straight at me with an intense expression.

"What did he want? What did he say? Why did he come here?" Caleb was always so calm and level-headed that the sequence of questions made me smile nervously.

"He was only here for a minute."

"What did he say?" Caleb asked.

I gave a shy shrug. "He heard about us getting married," I said.

I thought Caleb had been tense before, but I felt him physically tighten when I said that. "He was trying to get you back," he said as more of a statement than a question.

"No, not really," I said.

"What'd he say, *all the best?*"

"No," I said, with a humorless laugh. "But he wasn't trying to get back with me. He just said he was worried that I would... that he thought it was a mistake for me to get married so soon."

Caleb scoffed, shaking his head and looking irritated.

"Are you mad?"

"Yes, I'm mad. Did you know he was coming here?"

"No, he just showed up. He had heard about us and he came here because he thought I was..."

I was about to say marrying you out of desperation, but that was so off-base that I couldn't bring myself to say it.

"He thought you were what?" Caleb asked.

"He thought we were rushing into it, that's all. He thought there was no way we could be sincere."

"Did you set him straight?" Caleb asked, staring into my eyes with a smile that was patient and playful.

I smiled back at him. "Yes, I did," I said. "I told him he had no idea what he was talking about."

"You did?"

I nodded. "But I can't help but worry about all those other people who are like him—the ones who'll think we're making a mistake—going too fast."

"Do you think we are?" he asked, sincerely.

"No!" It was my honest answer, and the promptness of it made him smile.

"Do you think we're doing anything wrong in the eyes of God by falling in love and getting married?"

"No."

"So, it's basically just people you're worried about."

"Yes. I guess."

"Do you know that we're unable to control the things other people think?"

"Yes. I do know that. But it still bugs me."

"Do you know what the Bible says about things that bug you?"

"No, what?"

"It says *let not your heart be troubled.* It doesn't say that your heart will never be troubled. It says you have to not let it happen. You have to have to be an active participant."

"How am I supposed to do that?"

He shrugged. "People have different ways of letting go of things and giving them over to God. I like to picture leaving it on a gray space."

"Gray?"

"Yeah."

"Like fog? Or a gray room?"

"No, more like a pedestal, an area, a platform. Mine's just this gray platform. It doesn't really matter what it is, some people could probably make this same mental connection without picturing anything, but I see it in my mind as a round, flat, gray surface. It's nondescript. It's just a physical surface for me to picture so I can imagine lying down whatever's worrying me. It's the place where I hand it over to God in my mind. I see it up there, and whatever it is, I'm letting go of it."

I took a deep breath, feeling calmed somewhat by his suggestion. "I don't want people to think you're crazy, though."

"Who would say that?" he asked, furrowing his eyebrows. "Who would even *think* it?"

"It was the conversation with Liam that made me say that. He had come here thinking I was in serious need of an intervention."

"What happened, Stella? What did he say to you?"

Caleb knew me well enough to see that I was preoccupied, and he was insightful and persistent enough to figure out what was bothering me. I should just come out and say it.

"He just said it was silly of us to get engaged so quick. I don't care about it for myself," I said, explaining. "I just know how people talk. I'm thinking about you and your parents."

He held me close to him with his arms around my waist. "Was he mean to you today?" he asked.

"Who, Liam? No," I said. "I-I mean, no. He was just trying to—"

He stared at my face. He tilted his head and looked at me thoughtfully. "Did he make you cry?"

That was pretty much the last thing I expected him to say, so I didn't know what to do besides answer honestly. "Yes. But it wasn't because he was being mean. I was just... mad. He... people seem to pity you when they think you found God. It's like they think you've become different—weaker—which couldn't be further from the truth. But anyway, I tried not to waste too much time thinking about it once he left. Like I said, my concern is for you. Our friends are going to think different things, and I have a feeling you're going to get an even harder time than I am."

"First off, Stella. I want to be with you and you want to be with me. We've established that. I want to marry you, I've never been so sure of anything in my life. I think we can both agree that we're where we need to be when we're with each other."

He looked at me for confirmation, and I nodded. It was definitely true.

"We are doing nothing to go against what God would want in our lives," he said. "Both of us feel like God wants us to be together, right?"

I nodded.

"So I honestly don't care what anyone else thinks. Let them say what they're gonna say. We'll prove them wrong when we get old together."

"We will?" I asked.

He nodded. He was staring at me, smiling, holding me in his arms like I was his prize. "I don't see why we can't—" He paused but then continued. "I would leave right now and take you to Vegas if you want me to. We would get in my truck and drive to the airport without packing a stitch of clothing. We could be married by tomorrow. Maybe even tonight. It's earlier there than it is here."

Caleb was a hundred percent serious. I stared at him, feeling suddenly wound up by the fact that he was not kidding around.

"You would do it," I said, speaking quietly to him—flirting with him.

I drew closer to him and reached up to touch his cheek. My fingertips grazed the edge of his stocking cap.

"I would most certainly do it," he said. "I hate the fact that he was here. I am jealous. So jealous, Stella."

"You have nothing to worry about," I promised. "The whole time, all I could think about was... I only thought about other things."

"Only thought about what?"

I smiled. "Don't make me say it."

"But it's true though, huh? That you were thinking about me?"

I nodded. "Of course it's true," I said. I rested my forehead on his chest. "All I could think about was you," I said. "Maybe I have gone crazy, Caleb, because that plan about going to Vegas seems like a logical option. A good choice."

He looked at me with a serious, challenging expression that had an edge of mischief.

"Say that again, Stella, and see what happens. Say that going to Vegas sounds like a logical choice."

"What will happen if I say it?"

"I will, a hundred percent, take you there. I am entirely serious. I will not hesitate. I'm ready. I'll marry you and then we'll come back here and buy a house and a dog and have babies."

"In that order?" I asked, laughing a little and barely taking in what he was saying on account of my nerves.

"Yes, Stella, in that exact order. Don't even try me, because I will do it. I would love to do it."

"So all I have to do is say the word, and you'll take me to Vegas and marry me?"

Caleb nodded seriously. "Just like I said," he said. "I won't even go home. You could maybe pack a few things while we're here."

"You could throw some of Tanner's stuff in my bag," I said.

My whole body was alive with adrenaline.

It was an absolute insane thing for us to be discussing, and somehow it felt reasonable, logical, almost necessary.

Chapter 20

This moment was so much like a dream that it almost felt like I was swimming. The air was thick with emotion and excitement. The sun was setting, and we were standing in my parents' driveway deciding whether or not to run away to Vegas. It seemed as though both of us were leaning toward going, which was completely unbelievable and surreal.

Caleb leaned in and kissed me.

It was chilly out, but he held me tightly and his mouth was soft and warm against mine. In those seconds, there was no doubt in my mind that I should marry him. His mouth softened and molded to mine, and I gripped him tightly as I experienced a surge of desire. I wanted him. The physical desire was like nothing I had experienced with Liam. But it wasn't just physical with Caleb. I wanted to be his bride. He was right when he said we would grow old together. I could feel in my bones that I would be with him forever, that our love would be unwavering, that spending my life with Caleb was the right thing to do.

He knew it too because he proceeded to kiss me in a way that was not typical of standing in my parents' driveway. Caleb apparently didn't care where we were because he held me and kissed me tenderly, giving his attention to me and only me.

He pulled back and smiled a little bit before kissing me again, this time it was deeper and more intense. He opened his mouth and I felt his tongue slide against my lips as he kissed me, covered me, claimed me.

Caleb controlled the movement and rhythm of the kiss, and for an unknown amount of time, I was completely lost—relishing the warm velvety feel of his mouth. I knew I was the only person Caleb had ever given himself to in this way, and I was eternally grateful for that. Being with someone so pure was a gift.

He held me and kissed me, and I just stood there and took it all in. Physically, he was masculine and sturdy, and I took comfort in relinquishing control to him. No one was looking, but Caleb kissed me like he didn't care who saw. He held me and stared at me like he was completely oblivious to the world around us.

I knew he was sincere in his offer to marry me immediately, and there was just no way I could deny him. I would marry him tonight. I buzzed with anticipation, knowing I was about to agree and therefore action would be taken. I felt as if I was standing on the edge of a cliff, like some dramatic changes were about to happen in my life.

Caleb broke the kiss, smiling a little before leaning in to kiss me again. "Can you tell I'm trying to talk you into it?" he said lazily between kisses.

"You don't have to," I whispered.

Caleb pulled back, focusing on me, his expression growing serious. His eyebrows furrowed, and I grinned at his intensity. "What are you saying, I don't have to?"

"You don't have to try to talk me into it because I already want to—well, only if you're serious. I would say yes to leaving with you if you want to."

"I am serious," he said, nodding. "I'm ready. I don't even need to go home. I'll leave straight from here. We'll figure out the rest on the road."

My smile broadened. "We can pack you some of Tanner's stuff."

He nodded.

"But your dad's a pastor," I said as soon as I had the thought. "Couldn't we just get him to do it?"

"We could," he said. "I thought about that before I mentioned Vegas. I'm actually not sure how quickly it can happen here. Maybe by tomorrow." He brought his hand to the side of my face, gently touching my hairline. "It's up to you," he said. "We could do it like normal people and wait months or years. Or we could do it next week or tomorrow. Wait as long as you feel comfortable. Why don't we take Elmo for a walk and you can think about it?"

He started to let go of me, but I held onto him. I wasn't going to let him let me off the hook so easy.

"Or we could just go," I said.

"Yes, we could," he agreed, nodding and looking at me like he was entirely serious. Then he smiled. "Can we?" He was excited. I could see his wheels turning and I loved the way he grinned absentmindedly as he considered. "I don't know what kind documents we need to have, but if it's just a driver's license, I have that with me. And it's perfect timing, really. We're both still on Christmas break."

"I know. I already thought about that. And I don't think we need anything but a driver's license. We can go inside and look it up. It wouldn't be a big deal to stop by your apartment if you needed anything else."

Caleb nodded thoughtfully, agreeing with me.

"My dad has a bunch of airline miles from taking Tanner all over the place with AAU," I added. "I bet we can use some of those so it won't be so expensive."

"I really don't care to how much it costs," he said. Caleb glanced around like he was going to make a plan. "Are your parents home? Are they going to be okay with us doing this?"

I shook my head. "Dad's not home, but Mom is, and she knows more about all the airline stuff than Dad does. She would help us get tickets. And, yes, they'll be fine with it." Then I corrected myself, "I'm not sure if they'll be okay with it or not. They might have some words to say about it. Your parents probably would too. I guess we will have to tell them what we're doing and see what they say."

Caleb and I walked toward the house together. His arm was around my shoulders and mine was around his waist. I was walking on clouds, feeling like I was on top of the world as we broke apart and went into the house.

"Hey Caleb!" Mom yelled from the kitchen.

"Hello, Ms. Sara. It smells delicious in here."

"Well, thank you. Ricky put it together earlier. I'm just over here stirring it."

"What is it?"

"Beef stew. It's ready anytime if you're hungry, but I thought we'd wait for Ricky and Tanner. They'll be home in about an hour or so."

Caleb and I glanced at each other.

We were both thinking the same thing.

"Mom, I don't know if we'll... be here in an hour," I said.

"Where are you going?" she asked, glancing at me with a curious expression. She was standing over the stew, stirring it absentmindedly, but she was looking straight at me.

I'll let out a little nervous laugh as I said, "Vegas."

"Where?" She wore a comically curious expression. "Caleb's?"

"Vaa-gaas," I repeated, pronouncing it loud and clear.

Mom tilted her head. "What Vegas?"

"*Las* Vegas."

Her face somehow grew even more confused.

"Las Vegas, *Nevada*?"

I glanced at Caleb for a little reassurance. He saw me do it even though he was mostly looking at my mom. I saw the hint of a reassuring smile touch his mouth. I looked at my mom who was still appearing confused—maybe even a little cautious, wary. I watched as things started to sink in with my mother. The bad thing was that she didn't look very happy about it. I felt like I had to say something to lighten the mood.

"Sara, when two people love each other very much, sometimes they want to get married." I was being playful in hopes of getting her to smile.

"I hope you're not trying to go to Las Vegas to get married, Stella Claire."

She was not joking around.

She was not smiling.

She was entirely serious.

She did not spare a glance at Caleb.

She glared at me.

My heart pounded.

She just stared straight-faced at me, waiting for me to answer.

"Yes, Mom, I am trying to go to Las Vegas and get married."

"No, no, no, no, no, Stella." She was so fixed and serious that my eyes instantly began burning like I was about to cry.

"Please don't," she begged.

I instinctually held on tighter to Caleb since I didn't want her disapproval to push him away. I could not believe my mother was acting this way right in front of him. I was shocked. I thought my parents wholeheartedly supported me marrying Caleb. I thought she knew we wanted to do it sooner than later. Mom continued speaking, explaining herself, but those seconds were so painfully awkward that they seemed to take an eternity.

"Please don't leave here and do it without us, Stella." Her gaze shifted to Caleb. "Caleb, pleeease." She put her hands out before we could say anything to deny her. "I think you should get married whenever you want. Today, tomorrow, next week, whenever. Just don't do it without us. Surely you can do it here so we can all be a part of it."

Caleb and I turned to look at each other somewhat stiffly. It seemed as though we were equally stunned.

"Please," she said when she saw us hesitating. "Were you going to say that you were leaving right now for Las Vegas?"

I nodded.

"Tonight?" she clarified.

I nodded again, and she shook her head. "We knew you two were going to do this. I've already talked to Dad about it and we mentioned it to Tim and Catherine, too." She looked at Caleb. "We figured it was just a matter of time before you were calling up your daddy asking him to run up to the church and marry y'all at the drop of a hat. We thought we'd have to throw something together real fast. But *Vegas*? Stella Claire. That didn't even cross our minds. Surely y'all weren't thinking of sneaking off and not letting us celebrate with you."

Her face was so shocked and serious that I couldn't help but smile nervously. "We were," I said. "But it wasn't anything personal. It was just because we want to do it fast. We were trying to make it happen tonight."

"Can you please give me twelve hours to whip something up. Maybe twenty-four, but we'll do it fast. One day. You can give me one day, right?" She glanced at her wrist even though there was no watch on it. "I can have you married by this time tomorrow."

Mom was so on-the-spot with her elopement intervention that Caleb and I didn't have the heart to reject her offer.

"We can have it at Uncle E's," she said. "Some won't be able to make it on short notice, but most people will be able to come. People probably won't have much going on between Christmas and New Year's."

It was a skill I never knew she possessed, but my mother was willing, and happy to plan and execute an impromptu wedding. She must have really been prepared for it, because the wedding she put together happened the following afternoon at 4pm, and it was almost as big and as good as other weddings I had been to recently.

We did it in the afternoon because my brother had a basketball game at 7pm, and we wanted to make sure he could attend.

There were approximately seventy people in attendance at the wedding, and quite a few of them would leave afterward to watch my brother's game.

It was unbelievably perfect considering how spur of the moment it was. There was music, flowers, and strings of lights. Dinner was lasagna and salad prepared by a local restaurant, and my cousin's wife, who was a pastry chef, put together a beautiful wedding cake.

I went to the store that morning and bought a simple white dress off of the rack at the mall—nothing fancy—no lace or sequins. It was a simple, white, long-sleeved dress that had a plunging v-shaped neckline and a belt. I paired it with nude heels that matched perfectly.

Caleb went and got a fresh haircut, and he looked unbelievably dashing in his perfectly fitted navy suit. It was tailored and had the faintest of pinstripes and I have never seen him wear something so handsome.

His dad preformed the ceremony, and it was quick and funny but heartfelt. All of it came together seamlessly. Everybody who attended was loving and supportive and didn't, even for a second, question whether or not we were ready for marriage. If

198

anyone had thoughts or feelings of a negative sort, they did a great job of hiding them.

It was a celebration, a party. I felt like a princess. I was happier than I could have ever dreamed.

Thank goodness we didn't go to Vegas.

Epilogue

What were we thinking, you might ask, going to a high school basketball game on our wedding night?

The answer was simple. Caleb and I both really enjoyed Tanner's games and we didn't want to miss it. Up until this point, we hadn't really done things like most couples, so we figured why start now?

We finished up with our ceremony at Uncle E's and went straight to the school for the game. Tanner always had a big cheering section, but tonight there were more of us than usual. Even Caleb's family came. My mother had called ahead, and one of her friends held a section for thirty of us. The crowd was eager to let her do it since Uncle E would be there with us and he was such a legend. The whole school loved it when he showed up to games.

My dad, Caleb's dad, Uncle E, and Caleb went to the locker room when we arrived to give the team a pre-game talk and pray with them. Those of us who didn't go with them went into the stands where we took up a three-row section in the bleachers.

I sat on one end of the middle row, surrounded by my family. I had put on a coat and boots, but I still had on my white dress from the wedding. It was casual enough that I got away with wearing it without drawing stares. Maybe people did stare and I just didn't notice. Either way, I felt comfortable and happy being there in that packed gym.

It was a perfect thing to do on our wedding night. I was surrounded by people I knew and loved, and I was looking forward to watching my brother play. It was fun to watch someone you know play sports, but it's even better when they're really good at it. Tanner was good. He was the leader of this team, and they were winning games left and right. It would surprise no one if we were state champions this year. Caleb enjoyed it as much as I did, so both of us agreed that we wanted to come.

I was thinking about him at the moment because the guys were walking through the gym, headed our way. The problem was that Caleb was not with them. None of the other gentlemen seemed to be alarmed by his absence, so I knew there wasn't a problem, but I missed him and was ready for him to come sit beside me. I had saved him a place near the aisle.

My uncle sat in his seat.

"I just wanted to tell you..." Uncle E said, looking over his shoulder to make sure we weren't being overheard. "I love your husband."

I smiled and shook my head at him. I had no idea what he was going to say, and the simple declaration struck me as funny.

"I do," he said. "I don't have any girls, but I feel like my nieces are my own. You and Livi are important to Aunt Rhonda and me. It means a lot to us that you found a good man. It's important, and Caleb's a real good one. And he loves you. You should have heard him in there talking about you."

"What'd he say?" I asked.

Uncle E smiled. "I'm not telling you. That's a locker room secret. But it was good. He loves you. He's a good speaker, too. He had them all laughing. I said a few words before he got up there, and I'm glad I didn't have to follow him."

"Did he say we got married?" I asked.

"Yes, he did," Uncle E said. "Everybody clapped."

I felt myself smiling and blushing as I imagined that. "Where is he?" I asked, distracting him and myself.

"He stayed back to talk to Jimmy Whitmore's dad." Jimmy was one of the players on Tanner's team. I didn't know what business his father would have with Caleb, but it didn't matter. I knew Caleb would get there as soon as he could.

"Thank you for letting us do the wedding at your house tonight," I said. "And for everything. Mom told me you and Aunt Rhonda paid for the food."

He patted my shoulder in the familiar way uncles do. "It was our pleasure, baby girl. Seriously, I'm so proud of you. I think you did good with Caleb. Honestly, there are not too many men on the face of this earth that I would be this excited about you being with."

"He's a good one, huh?" I asked, leaning into my uncle.

"So good."

"There he comes," I said, watching as Caleb came out through the double doors that led into the gym. He knew where we normally sat, and it only took him a few seconds to find me.

"I'm gonna go sit by Rhonda," Uncle E said, patting my shoulder again to say goodbye. He got to the edge of the bleachers. "You kids have fun tonight," he said as he stood. He was smiling as he moved to sit on the other side of my mother where a spot was being saved for him. I had glanced his way when I heard my name from below.

"Congrats, Stella!"

It was a guy's voice coming from the basketball court. One of the players, Jaden Thomas, was waving at me. Warmups had begun and he took the time to shout at me while was waiting in line for the ball. I waved and blew him a kiss, and several of the other guys standing around took a cue from him and congratulated me from the floor. There was music and noise and action, and I could not stop smiling.

Caleb climbed the bleachers, crossing the space between us quickly, and before I knew it, he was coming to sit beside me.

The first thing he did was lean over and kiss my cheek. "This was a mistake," he said.

His tone was lighthearted but serious and I pulled back to stare at him curiously.

"Coming here... first," he explained. "It was a mistake." He was speaking into my ear and only loud enough for me to hear.

I pulled back to regard him curiously. "What happened?" I asked using the same low volume.

"Nothing happened. And I'm good with staying. But you're so beautiful, and I guess I didn't factor that coming here would mean there would be a couple of hours where I have to remain... calm." He hesitated before he said that last word, calm, and he said it dramatically, making me laugh a little.

"Are you telling me you're going be hyper later?"

"No," he said, wearing an irresistible smile. "But maybe," he added with a shrug. "I don't really know what I'll do."

"You'll be perfect," I said, leaning in and speaking right next to his ear. I did it on purpose.

"Don't," he said.

"Don't what?" I asked.

"You probably shouldn't whisper in my ear like this unless you feel like leaving early."

I leaned over to whisper in his ear again. "I heard the butterflies are the best part," I said. "Those moments where your heart's racing."

I leaned toward him so that I could put my hand discreetly on the side of his leg. Then I remembered everything Uncle E had just told me and I smiled and whispered to him again.

"I love you, and I'm proud of you," I said.

I said it in my sweetest most sincere voice with my mouth next to his ear. I felt him grab a fist full of my clothing behind my back as he otherwise casually leaned in to whisper back to me.

"We'll try to stay till the half," he said.

His voice was doubtful, and I smiled at him for being in such a rush.

The truth was that I was in a rush, too, but I liked these moments of build-up and I felt grateful for the simple pleasure of sitting next to a man like Caleb.

In most cases, happily ever after was as much as a person could ask for, but from where I stood, the phrase seemed like an understatement.

The End
(till book 4)